MASON

MASON

US VERSUS THE WORLD

RACE WALTERS

MASON
US VERSUS THE WORLD

iUniverse books may be ordered through booksellers or by contacting:

iUniverse
1663 Liberty Drive
Bloomington, IN 47403
www.iuniverse.com
1-800-Authors (1-800-288-4677)

ISBN: 978-1-5320-9368-5 (sc)
ISBN: 978-1-5320-9369-2 (e)

Library of Congress Control Number: 2020901136

Print information available on the last page.

iUniverse rev. date: 01/22/2020

PROLOGUE

Thousands of years ago, long before the existence of humans, an Earthly species called the empowered began to rise, a race similar to humans today. These beings developed with odd quirks that the world hadn't seen yet, usually linked to unstable genetics and rapid, extreme evolution. Over the years, these beings gained attributes like extreme speed and endurance, but in some rare cases, their traits went as far as having the capability of changing matter and energy. Over time, most of the empowered matured into separate classes. Those, however, who were less fortunate began to suffer from odd, unexplainable changes. They began to flicker in and out of existence; painful strains transmuted their figure and destroyed the atoms that structured their bodies.

The empowered that were steady and grounded in reality became classified as surreals; beings with powers that changed the tangible world. These included talents like clairvoyance, elemental bending, and governing energy. The empowered that were able to affect time, the planes of existence, and space around us were deemed ethereals. For those who avoided their self-destruction, ethereals collected skills that functioned behind reality, skills that allowed them to see inside the aether.

Over hundreds of years, the surreals spread out and their genetic makeup began to evolve based on their surroundings. Ethereals, at this point, were rare to come across. Their numbers were few and far between, and even those alive tended towards isolation.

Ethereals, like us, began to sharpen their focus so that they could organize their scrambled thoughts and exponential stress. Throughout the generations, we learned how to function normally again.

Until people started going hungry.

Over time, as populations grew, food, resources, and land all became sparse. The surreals watched with fear and anger as the ethereals tried to live amongst them. When the overbearing tension finally reached its breaking point, war broke loose. The two types of empowered burst out into a mad slaughter. A disgusting battle, a nightmarish crusade for survival amongst the starving.

In the wake of destruction, a secluded group of neutrals, surreals and ethereals alike, decided to create a single race that could walk the Earth in harmony. No special power, no uncommon abilities, each one would be the same. Together, over the course of years and underneath the surface, they created the first biological lifeforms we know of today as the humans. This day, the day humans were created, was deemed as year 0.

This subterranean group of empowered, later named the Scholars, tried to keep the race hidden away from the war; the humans were fragile, much less powerful than any others. Those in the massacre outside didn't agree with this new breed of beings. Some of the first humans ever exposed were quickly destroyed civilizations that contradicted the Scholars' beliefs. They were quickly outlawed and hunted down, forced beneath the surface again. Years passed before the bloodshed finally came to a conclusion. Devastation reigned across the world, the survivors were the minority. Death and disease ravaged the new world, few persevered through the apocalypse. The only ones alive were few aggressors, the shrinking body of surviving Scholars, and the new race that was constructed by the empowered, the humans. A new force called mankind.

Gifted with fake history and fake memories of their past, the humans were ready to take over. Humans quickly began to outnumber and overtake the others. In order to survive, the empowered cloaked themselves inside the human populace; most of the Scholars either joined them in hiding or failed to keep existing. Finally, after the world had been overrun, all we were left with were the humans and a small number of us.

The number of those who had power dwindled more and more. With an explosion of growth, the human population began to spread across the globe. For a while, humans and the empowered bred; although, surreals are incompatible with humans. Ethereals, on the other hand, could have offspring with humans to create what are called half-ethereals, ethereals that share only some diluted abilities with us. But after a while, all interbreeding ceased as the empowered became afraid of the countless powerless. At some point, the empowered took their faces out of the history books. Forever.

Years and years later, the world was fully colonized and totally healthy again. The war that happened long ago was long since forgotten, and the knowledge of the existence of supernatural beings was forever buried with those who died in combat.

When I was growing up I learned that we, the nonhumans, are being constantly stalked, sought after, and murdered by the hands of transgressors.

There's nothing more disgusting to me than taking a life, especially those of the innocent.

I've only ever found surreals; I've never met another ethereal in my life, I long for the day when I have the fortune to. I hold dear the chance to meet another one like me, meet one of my own. Since the day I was born, I've felt ropes tied around me, little strings held up by invisible hands. Every day of my life, I feel the others tugging on these ropes, pulling me towards them, asking me to greet them. Day after day, night after night, they talk in my head, relentless and hysterical.

But every time I try to follow the ropes, I get caught on something.

Tied up in a mess I can't get out of; protecting someone I shouldn't care about. Kids, adults, the weak, the powerful; all of them are the same in the end. I don't know them. They keep their secrets to them, I'll keep mine to myself.

But Rose found out, and now she's told the others.

CHAPTER I

ME AND TWO OTHERS

I can hear you even better. I bet that means it's getting stronger, we must be getting closer!

Over and over, the voices keep sounding in my head. They're getting excited over the idea of their encounter.

It's odd, I can't find it within myself to explain my feelings; I don't know who any of them are, I've never even heard any of their *true* voices. Yet, despite all that, it's almost like I can feel their heartbeat better than my own. I can feel each one of them tugging on me. Drawing me to them, or pulling them toward me.

I think that this is my family, and they're reaching out for me from somewhere.

In a big, empty gym room, upstairs in the facility, I sit, hunched over on a bench as I watch the kids train. They practice battling with each other, laughing and chatting in between sessions. From where I sit, I can see lights flashing and purple mist flying across the room. Laughter swallows the sound of battle, bright rays spark like fireworks.

As I watch flares and shadows fly, a single blast makes its way in my direction. With a splatter it lands between my feet. The ball of acid slowly begins to eat away at the laminated floor. Smoldering and simmering, the laminated flooring seems to shriek, while the hole grows. I don't flinch. Rather, I examine. The flooring once shiny is now eaten away, leaving a hole, like a bite out of a shiny fruit. The floor is battered and beaten by this practice battle, but around me, there's still some left untouched.

Surrounding the now burned flooring I catch a distorted view of myself in an untouched section of floor. Is this what I am now? Something me, yet not? What have I been doing for so long? It's so hard to remember who I've become.

My hair has grown much too long; if I let it down it would surely reach my eyes. I sweep it back and to the side. It's curly and greasy and begging to be cut. My grey eyes have grown tired, dark bags beginning to show. The scars across my face are almost healed, brown facial hair has begun to creep across my jaw. My leather jacket, years old at this point, like me, is showing a hard life; my name, Mason, is embroidered above the chest pocket. My white t-shirt is dirty and yellow around the collar, jeans are worn out and tattered around the knees, the soles of my tennis shoes are thinning out already even though it's only been a few months since I got them.

On the under-side of my wrist is a tattoo of a silver dragon. A tattoo that haunts me. Its silver etching shimmers in the light. Although the dragon has no eye I can feel it staring at me, burning holes in my heart, suffocating me. The redness around my wrist has gone away since the tattoo's creation but the scars haven't faded.

My face has grown tanned from being out in the warm weather and bruises once there faded long ago. I tug on my collar revealing a scar on my neck, now, barely visible. A scar from a burn in the shaped like lightning seared my skin. The burn from electric shock. The shock and scar due to Logan's stupidity, no surprise.

Another bolt of acidic violet matter burns a hole right where I was looking. These three teenagers have been burning images into my head for months now; I can't think of anything but their faces, their actions, anymore. I go home, wake up, come here; rinse and repeat. Every single day. Eating up my time, eating up my entire damn life. Three supernatural kids that I can't get off of my nerves. All I see anymore are these impulsive, reckless, idiotic, selfish children. When I came here for the first time, I decided that I wanted to help, do whatever it takes to stop them from walking in my shoes. Never did I mean to pick the three most unbearable, relentless delinquents in existence.

Logan, a 15-year-old boy, too full of himself with an oversized ego. With skills as yet untrained, he talks a big story, but has nothing to actually show us. In practice, his stance waivers, his hands shake. For some unknown reason, he acts like he's the guardian of the group; like if the world was coming to an end, he'd be in the front of the picture protecting those beneath him. In reality, he's nothing, yet I try teaching, hoping he will learn. Logan's skin is pale, showing off bruises on his forehead and arms, bruises gained from hard practice. He has short, dark hair, and brown eyes hidden by a pair of thin-frame prescription sunglasses. Logan is a mix, an athletic body, but no muscle or fat to fill him out, but his chest is wide, giving him a top-heavy look. Emotionally, mentally, and physically he's weak; absolutely pathetic in my opinion.

Logan is a magnus and is able to warp energy around himself, usually in the form of electricity. Magnusses are powerful, capable of many things, even teleportation. He has the ability to mold energy around him in tactical, spectacular ways but he generally just shocks himself and, on most days, me. He is learning his power and for now it is too untested for him to expel energy very far from his body, so he generally just uses his talents as fancy taser hands to shock anybody he touches. Although, if that person just so happens to touch him back, he'll receive the same voltage, same shock. He has a future that includes the use of light and sound, even nuclear energy, but he hasn't figured any of those out. If he listens and learns, I may be able to show Logan all he is capable of.

Victoria, a 14-year-old girl, is an absolute nuisance. A little brat with the overwhelming desire to complain. She has a quick temper, her impulsiveness is disgusting, and could lead to someone, even her, getting hurt. Victoria lacks any kind of maturity, lacks self-control, has a big mouth with no filter, and for me is the most irrational and irritating kid in the group. She has chosen to shave one side of her head, and leave the rest of her dark, curly hair to hang, concealing half of her face. Her grey eyes, similar to mine but bigger, are windowed by thick glasses. Her hands are wrapped in black lace gloves, fitting in with the emo attire that she refuses to live without. Her clothes are always dark and depressing to look at; fitting of such a witch.

Victoria has control over shadow material, an acidic clay-like substance that she can create and mold into weaponry or airborne projectiles. At high speeds it can get painful; I would know, it's on me often enough. Her limited experience makes it troublesome for her to shoot with high velocity or accuracy, but she is learning

She also has the ability to "whisper"; a skill used by mischieviants to influence other's decisions by getting in their head and speaking to them in a demonic tongue, similar to a succubus. This influence grows stronger the closer she gets. If someone is touching her while she whispers her influence is unstoppable.

Rose, a 12 year old, mouse-like girl, is the hardest one to get to know. She's irritating nonetheless, but not a nuisance like the others. She has large, bright blue eyes, filled more times than not, with fear. She has no idea how to deal with stressful situations, the smallest amount of tension breaks her like a toothpick. Whenever I ask her to do anything during her training she hesitates, making practice go on and on, or she flat out refuses to try. I understand being timid, but her levels of anxiety are outrageous. Her long platinum-blonde hair is beautiful and in most girls would add confidence to their being. Her beauty as a young girl makes her look like she could take on the world, when in reality there's not much of anything she can truly take on at all.

Behind her timid facade is a brilliant visioneer, a species capable of some of the most powerful mind tricks any species can pull off. As a visioneer, she is a genius, and is able to not only read, but study the minds of others. What she lacks in confidence she makes up in pure intelligence. No puzzle too difficult, and surprisingly, puzzles and high-concentration scenarios seem to bring out her talents. It is astonishing to watch her, her potential and abilities gain strength, especially if she forgets she is not alone. Then she becomes a brilliant star. As a reflex, when danger nears, she can turn invisible, clothes and all. Not sure how she affects the things around her, but she does it. Although, during her invisible state, light can't bounce off of her retinas so she's rendered totally blind. She hasn't learned how to work with this disability so she generally runs into things or makes loud noises, completely giving away her position.

We've been training for weeks on end and yet so little progress has been made. It's stupendously difficult to teach these kids; I don't understand them. I don't get what makes them tick, why they won't listen, why they won't learn anything I try to teach them. My stress levels are always at their limits when I'm here. *Why* am I here? I keep asking myself, but never have I found an answer, and return day after day

When I came here for work, they offered me a position training kids how to use their powers. It's part of the facility's practice, teaching kids simple academics and how to use their abilities without harming themselves. Little did I know, I would get the troubled students.

Once, long ago, I wanted to be a hero. I wanted to be the one who persevered and helped the world be better. My gruesome past is filled with misery and sadness, why should anybody ever follow in my footsteps? If I could prevent others from suffering the way I did, why would I turn my cheek, how could I just look away?

It only took months to realize that my dreams were made to be crushed as the world is much bigger than I am. I can't save anybody, much less everybody. I'm stuck in a trap created by my old mindset, constantly in the danger I put myself in. There's no need to give anybody any high expectations. I'll save myself and I'll be happy, nobody else matters.

Most people don't deserve my sacrifices, anyways.

I don't care about anybody other than myself. The only thing that should matter to me, the only thing that *does* matter to me, is my own well-being. There's no reason for me to be stressing over anybody other than Mason.

Yet, I still sit here, watching my life wither away in front of the only adolescents who don't understand how instructions work. As I watch, I wish that it'll get easier; I wish that one day these kids would wake up and understand everything I'm saying. Maybe one day, they'll awaken and suddenly understand the point I'm trying to get across. The point that their lives are at risk, as well as those of the ones around them.

Not that they ever will, though.

I know that life doesn't always get easier. I try to train these three kids with what knowledge I have of their powers. I only know general fighting and brief summaries of what they can do. I don't have any of their abilities, so I'm doing the best I can by using the knowledge I gained while learning to control my abilities. What I know is combat, tactics, things that will assist one in battle. I've never been able to shock things or read minds, I can't do anything that fancy. All I can teach is poise and battle strategy; though, I've realized that teaching a handful of young brick walls with giant mouths is much more challenging than I ever expected it to be.

I stand up, catching everybody's attention. Rose barely looks at me from the corner of her eye as she slowly reappears, her hands clutching herself in a small, mouse-like position. Victoria is sitting on the ground, her arms crossed, her expression angry. She looks bratty and upset, too stubborn to stand up. Logan is still trying to regain his footing after the last time he shocked himself. He looks like an uncoordinated drunk. With a heavy sigh, I explain a new plan as I watch each one of them take their place a couple of feet apart. I turn toward one corner, looking back at all of them as they murmur to each other. Rose stays away from them all; she doesn't need to speak, her actions do it for her.

I yell loud enough for them to hear me as I keep walking away, "Here's how it's gonna go."

I take a deep breath and think back.

I can't get it out of my mind. I've been here for months and they don't even have a clue.

Almost two months ago I learned that there was a facility called Eden Orphanage; a group that has taken it upon itself to raise kids like these, raise kids like *us*. Kids with powers. Somewhere they can stay safe, somewhere they won't be in danger, somewhere they don't have to be scared for their lives due to the defects they were born with. Being raised on the streets, I kept my abilities to myself because I was terrified, afraid of what the humans do to me.

Torture me? Humiliate me? Kill me?

I was the little boy who could run fast and smell blood; I never wanted to be the street-boy circus act, I wanted to be a kid. For the longest time, I didn't have anybody to protect me, anybody to keep me out of trouble. People said they cared but nobody ever really did.

There's something about these kids that appealed to me at first. Now I can't imagine what it was. Maybe it's because of the one thing they all shared: they were treated like outcasts by the other kids. Rose never strayed too far from the corner of the room. The staff has told me that she wasn't always that way, that there was something that made her that way, though she never told me what it was. All I knew was that she was constantly alone and cuddled amongst herself. Victoria's a total bitch to everybody, it's not a surprise that she's alone most of the time. Starting fights, arguing with staff, she's always in trouble, but she doesn't seem to enjoy it as much as she causes it. Whether she starts the battle or not, it's possible that she feels regret but is too stubborn to admit it.

When I first met her, I had a lot more sympathy for her, she always seemed so cute and lonely. From what I've seen now, she's far from being lonely or cute. Logan is extremely awkward and has no idea how to act around people, the kid has no social skills. His brother used to stay here as well; no idea why he doesn't anymore. Logan doesn't talk about it at all, but as far as I can guess, his brother did most of the talking for him.

I look at these castaway kids in front of me. The ones that don't know how to act and have no idea how to make friends. I'm shaking my head, all I can think about is myself; I guess I'm the same. I don't have any friends, I don't know how to talk to people, I hate people. I spend all my time with those that I can't stand, I go home every night and go to sleep by myself; alone in a small apartment with no connection to anybody else. I'm alone in my own little world. In the end, though, I don't care. Everybody else can screw up their own shit, I don't need them to help me.

I instruct them through some exercises, simple training for their powers. I keep some testing dummies in the storage room, human body punching bags with only a torso and head; no arms.

Logan works on trying to expel energy farther; rather than having to touch the target, he tries to use energy from a distance. The training dummy is made of rubber which is extremely resistant to electricity; I've cut a couple of holes in the shoulders and chest exposing the metal pole in the center. Metal attracts electricity pretty well, yet he's only able to reach about a foot of distance so far. I can hear his grunts as he tries to forcefully work his hands but with little success. I walk up behind him and put my hands on his shoulders making him jump. In a light whisper I tell him, "Your theatrical production is awful. Work on your acting skills." He stops, with an exasperated breath. I shake my head, "You shouldn't be tired so quickly. Quit overdoing it, this is easy." Refusing to look at me, he focuses on the dummy and makes a forced expression of concentration. He puts his hands up far in front of him and curls his fingers but I slap them down, "This isn't a movie. Stop exaggerating." Annoyed, he tries again, his hands and arms more relaxed but his facial expression still tense. I walk away, "Quit it." Logan growls at me but I don't respond.

Walking over to Victoria, I can see her flicking shadows at her dummy; every successful shot burning tiny pea-sized holes into the rubber. Her expression is careless and bored, she looks at me with disdain as she continues flicking. Every time her finger strikes her thumb, a small purple mass lobs away from her hand and arcs its way towards the dummy, usually missing. I scoff, "You know, if you actually *tried* a little, you might hit it."

She snickers at me, "You know, you have no idea what you're talking about."

"You know, I'm here for *you*, not for me," my voice raises a little.

"You know, nobody *wants* you here," she loudly sneers as she flicks one of her little shadow balls at me. I easily dodge her inaccurate attack.

I sigh with defeat shaking my head in disappointment, "You're pathetic." Looking back ever so slightly, I see a fire in her eyes. With a scoff, she flicks a quarter-sized ball at me, quicker but still slow enough for me to move out of its way with ease. I shake my head in disapproval. Quickly, she brings up her other hand and begins firing faster, rapidly sending airborne acid at me. Changing things up, she stops flicking them, and starts lobbing, throwing, chucking them.

As I dodge her attacks, I begin to circle her. About four feet away, I keep sliding around her, drawing an imaginary circle on the ground with my feet. As I continue my evasion, Victoria's expression gets angrier, her attacks get stronger and faster. After a couple of circles around her, Victoria finally yelps out in anger and pitches a tennis ball-sized blast aiming right between my eyes. Dropping my head down, the strike flies just above my scalp; I can feel the warm wind push my hair back. Behind me, I can hear the simmering of cooked rubber. I look behind me seeing a crater right where the dummy's nose used to be. I snicker, walking away from the injured punching bag. As I pass Victoria, I catch a glimpse of her face, totally consumed in awe. I pat her head as I walk away, "You'll get there, champ." She quickly yelps at me and slaps my hand away, I can't help but chuckle as I walk away from her.

The kids truly do irritate me, however it's very fun to push their buttons.

After a few minutes, the kids are actually trying to make progress. Victoria is tossing small strikes but with higher velocity and better accuracy. As she practices, her motions become more natural and of her own creation. Each shot is landing closer to the center of her target; with time she becomes more fluid. I'm sure in her mind, she put my face on the dummy. Logan is inching his way further away from his dummy. His body is more relaxed, his hand motions are more controlled, his theatre performance is slowing down, and his concentration is rising.

I sit down on the bench and look around, but I can't see Rose anywhere. I look to my left, there's no sign of her. Her training dummy is left totally vacant and untouched. I look to my right, only to catch her sitting inches away from me; I jump up in surprise. Her expression is somber as she looks down at her feet, swinging back and forth, her toes pointed towards each other. I relieve a deep sigh and sit back down. I look at her and speak quietly, "Why aren't you training, Rose?"

Rose doesn't respond. I'm not surprised, but something surely does seem different. I ask again, but more sternly "Rose, why aren't you training?"

She stays completely silent as she watches her feet swing backwards and forwards.

I look down and slouch over my legs, resting my elbows on my knees. Shaking my head, I sigh and rub my eyes with one hand, "Rose, I need you to-"

"Mason," she interrupts. I look at her quizzically, it's not often she talks, much less interrupts. I open my mouth to speak but she's ready to talk first. I am shocked. She's never spoken over me before. I pause for a moment, then finally sit back and rest my arm on the bench, "What is it?"

She sits silently, watching her swinging feet like there's a package on the ground that she doesn't want to open. She stops swinging her legs, the tension building like a balloon inflating inside a box. She takes a breath and asks, "I think I know too much, Mason."

I furrow my brows, confused. "W-what?" I ask, hesitantly.

She looks at me with the biggest, saddest eyes I've seen. Tears begin streaming down her soft cheeks, her small lips are trembling, "You're training us to fight because we may have to one day, aren't you? We aren't supposed to know, but there's someone out there, right? Somebody who wants us... Wants us..." She fails to finish her sentence before she bursts into a sob. I face her, looking for comforting words. Unfortunately, I don't know of any.

"Rose, no! It's not... That simple," I try. I scoff, annoyed and upset at my own stupidity and curiosity, "Listen, that's not what I meant... It's more like-" Her sobs become more intense.

I growl under my breath. Damn, I knew she was smart but this is too much. My disabled social skills have only confirmed it for her. If she knows that, what else does she know?

Suddenly, it clicks in my head. I get it now.

This girl must have been spending her whole life here with that knowledge. Plenty of adults here know, plenty of staff members know what's going on. If she can read minds, she's known this whole time that she's in danger, that something's pretty fishy about this place. Nobody has been there to comfort her because nobody else her age knows. If any adult here figured out she knew, who knows what they'd do? She doesn't tell anybody because she knows they'd be in her shoes if they knew. She doesn't speak because she cares.

Her sobbing calms down just enough to choke out some words, "You're going to kill me, aren't you, Mason? Aren't you one of them?"

My heart drops.

Inside my tiny mind, I lose it. My eyes widen and I choke. I try to think of something but she's too quick to reply, "Four years ago, my brother used to live here. He knew. He knew *everything*. He always had been the smartest one in the building and everybody knew. I could hear the staff members thinking things like 'He knows too much,' and 'We need to get rid of him.' Days passed before they told him that somebody wanted to adopt him, but nobody here has ever been adopted. This place isn't even *for* adoption. These kids don't know they're different, do they?" Her words become harsher as pain began to fill her throat, she speaks louder and faster, "We spoke to each other constantly. Mentally, from far away I could see what he saw."

This was all news to me. I had never heard of anything like adoption or the kids lacking knowledge; the gears in my head begin grinding away as I try to wrap my head around what's going on. Is this even the real Rose? How could she be so outgoing? A chill creeps up my spine as I listen.

"It was awful. Darkness, machinery, pain. Like his body was being hollowed out and replaced with something else," her words become a jumble as her sobs take over completely. Chills crawling up my back have taken me hostage, I feel paralyzed.

What the hell is this place? This is supposed to be a safe house for the empowered, not a prison. I try to get my thoughts around it but my brain scatters when I hear a cry from across the room, *"Mason!"*

I quickly look up seeing a large ball of purple ooze flying haywire in my direction. It would have been easy to dodge, but my eyes were so fixed on Rose that I didn't even react. It pelts my chest. Before I can even put my eyes on Victoria, I begin to feel a shocking sensation from it; it's like I'm wrapped in electrical wire, I can't tell what's going on. It takes all of my strength to turn my head and search for the culprit, but I can't seem to find one. Logan is yards away, he can't be doing this.

Did he charge this oozy shit? Like a *battery*?

I'm trying so hard to move but my muscles are too stiff, it's like they're wrapped in tight bandages. The pain intensifies as I try to move any part of my body; I funnel strength into my muscles but the effort returns minimal outcome. I can barely lift my arms, why is it shocking me for so long? I try to think about it but it feels like my brain is fried.

I can hear Rose in my head but there's no words, just sobbing. Utter disdain fills my head. She's not making me hear something, she's forcing her emotions on me.

Through the physical pain and vicarious emotional pains, I try to think; it obviously happened when Victoria struck me. Is it possible for Logan to charge her attacks somehow? Is shadow matter conductive? Can it hold electricity then emit it later? Seconds, minutes pass before I'm finally released from electrocution.

Toppling over, I hit the ground and begin panting. I look up, Victoria and Logan are both looking at me with the same expressions of total bewilderment. I furrow my brow at Logan and Victoria and shake my head as I try to stand up. I'm wobbly, but I get my stance coordinated, "You guys are *idiots!* What the *hell?*"

Victoria gives me a haughty grimace but I ignore her. I look over to Rose, but she's gone. I hear her somewhere, she's invisible but her still ragged breathing gives me enough to find her. I reach her, and drop to my knees, putting a hand where I think her shoulder is, "Rose! I need you to listen to me!"

As things settle down, I realize how breathless I am. Fatigue is consuming my body as I try to regain stability. Looking over, Logan stumbles on his feet, I'm seeing a couple of him right now, my vision is giving way.

I'm so dizzy; it feels like I'm about to collapse. The entire place is spinning in circles, I can't comprehend or understand what's going on. I'm so exhausted. I have been for so long.

As Rose slowly reappears I can see her making eye contact with me. The room starts orbiting me and the world begins to blur together, the question begins to bounce around my head, *where am I?* Voices echo at me, it feels like I'm dreaming. I think I'm passing out, I can't tell what's going on. My thoughts racing before I even realize Rose has slipped away and backed up. Fear penetrates our eye contact, her expression becomes awful, frightened and angered by me. I stumble to my feet as lethargy washes over. I try to stand up straight but my vision turns black and I topple over.

I can feel myself hitting the ground but I can't move and I don't feel pain. I can't see anything but I can count the seconds in my mind. I hear whispering in my head, dark voices and piercing eyes. *Find them.* Over and over, *bring them here.*

It's totally silent. When I finally come to, I prop myself up on my elbows and slowly open my eyes to look around. To either side of me is Victoria and Logan, both holding their hands up in childish, yet menacing poses. Rose is cowering in fear, backed against a corner of the room.

Now Rose knows, and she's told the others.

CHAPTER II

THE DEMONS THAT CONSUME ME

Dragon Technology Incorporated. A large scale industry that builds the most popular line of personal-use and at-home technology. They are world leaders of marketing and an underground company of killers.

Kids like Rose, Logan, and Victoria are in constant danger. There's so many villains in the world; people without consciences, greedy people who want to exploit the power of others. The evil ones are everywhere. These people are demons in suits and ties.

Except I wear a jacket and jeans, not a suit.

I joined them to stop them, so I could take advantage of their resources and fight. I was trained to be a scout, to search for the empowered, those who cause anomalies in the atmosphere. I was hired to capture them, bag them, and run them back home. What I really do, though, is use the chances they give me to hide those I am supposed to capture, keep them out of criminal hands and far off the radar.

At least, that's what I used to do.

For nearly two excruciating months I've been heading over to Eden Orphanage instead of scouting anomalies. I come here, train kids, help staff, then walk my ass home everyday. My bravery and courage slowly diminished as I saw how big the world is, how big the company is, and how small I am. Over time, my dreams and ambitions began to crumble beneath me. The only reason I still have work is because they believe I'm working on a huge case; I guess realistically, I am. I'm probably a danger to these kids.

Here I am, lying on the ground, surrounded by my failures. How stupid of me, trying to coach these delinquents. This wasn't my business and I never should have come here. My life hasn't gotten any better here, so why the hell come back? I'm risking my job and my life by being here; probably the life of the others as well. My boss isn't only after their heads but he's after mine, too. He may not know it yet, but he is.

Putting myself in the spotlight at work isn't a great idea for me. In fact, it's a terrible idea. I'm an ethereal, I radiate anomalies like a shooting star. Even in a group of non-humans, I'm like a Vegas billboard in the countryside. Here I am, though, sticking my neck out, making myself vulnerable in the wild.

The kids were meant to be trained and I took the lead, look where that got me. Rose sticks her grubby little paws in my head and tells everybody in the room that I'm a savage killer. Tells everybody I work for the bad guy when she has no idea what I do. To think I felt bad for her for even a damned second. The facility is extremely secure anyways, these kids never needed me and I never needed them.

I want privacy, time to think to myself. Around Rose, even my own head is being monitored.

I clear my head and jump to my feet as weakness inflicts my body. It feels heavy, everything hurts. I back away from Victoria but Logan catches the back of my head with a flat hand, holding my head down. Electricity suddenly flows through my body, quickly intensifying. I'm forced to take all of my power and funnel it into my strength. I have to grab him to relieve some of the pain.

I struggle; I'm worried at this point that my physical health might be on the line, I panic. My hand makes its way over to Logan, grabbing his bicep with the tightest grip I can manage; not very solid, but enough to hand off some of the shock. I hear him scoff at it but he's much too late to react.

Reinforcing my hold, I move my other hand down, reaching aimlessly in hope for a better hold. I barely get within brushing distance of his hip. Pain is surging through my body, I want to scream in agony but my vocal cords feel shot. The pain is unbearable, I can feel my heart beating so hard it's hurting my chest, my skin is reaching scorching levels of heat.

They say young snakes are the most dangerous because they lack control. They can spew venom, but they don't know how to stop. Logan is much like a young snake; and his fangs have sunk deep into my bloodstream.

Everything's a blur. Through my tears I see the others. Victoria is hazy but I can make out Rose hiding behind her. Agony constricts my joints even more creating unbearable tension in my body. There's nothing I can do.

But suddenly, he lets go.

I fall to the ground motionless, engulfed with pain and weakness. He may be afraid of pain but he held on for so long, I can smell his suffering; it kind of smells like charred flesh. Now that he can bring himself to speak, he's screaming. Although, his whales of agony fall on deaf ears, nobody can help him now. Louder, his cries pierce me. If I had any more pain to feel I'd yell, but I'm numb.

As the commotion settles down, he falls silent and goes totally limp.

I drop to my knees, my senses are everywhere and my mind is spinning. Next to me is the body of one of the cretins I was trying so hard to help. I look to Rose. My voice is shot, my body is in pain.

Think what you want, but I'm no killer.

I can see her reaction to my thoughts, she's scared of me. I'm sure she's reading my mind constantly, the little hag. My vision loses color, my sense of smell and hearing diminishes, the feelings in my nerves ceases. With the small bit of essence gathered from the loss in my abilities, I give myself the strength to pick him up.

This is part of my power; it's called bargaining.

I start making my way out of the gym. He doesn't deserve it, but I can't let him die. The infirmary is across campus, the walk may take a while. Whatever, once this kid is out of my hands, I'll be free to leave.

Rose opens her mouth and emits a light squeak. She's attempting to say something to me but I turn around and snap, *"Don't you dare say a word to me!"* My roar scares even Victoria as it echoes through the entire room. Rose turns invisible, the only thing I can see is her tears as they hit the ground. Visible or not, I can see her timid little stance, curled up like a mouse under a trap. I give them each a stern look, and then keep walking.

Don't you dare pretend like you know me. Don't you dare threaten my life without even a clue *of the truth.*

As I enter the more crowded areas outside the gym, people begin to look at me, kids and staff alike. I ignore all of them and keep walking.

This is the last time I help any of you.

Victoria and Rose don't move an inch. Standing hopeless in the middle of the gym, I can sense Rose's mind click. I can feel the sensation of her realizing what she's done; it's amazing. I almost pity her.

My footsteps are echoing in my head. The murmurs of the people around sound more like vague whispers than conversation. I can feel them gossiping about me, talking about me, spreading rumors about me. Hundreds of slow, measly steps take me to the infirmary. Through the main hall and out the building, pushing and shoving through large crowds of employees and children, I finally reach it: a small building designated for nursing and counseling, the "Health and Well-Being Center". Past the large, heavy double doors, I enter the first room on my right filled only with an old lady tapping away at her small laptop. She slowly turns to look at me, her beady brown eyes barely open and the corners of her lips curve down dramatically in a grimace. Her furrowed eyebrows show concern. I lay Logan on an open cot; the white paper lining crinkles and crackles under his weight. I close the curtains around his bed, cutting us off from the outside hall, "He hurt himself pretty bad." My voice is grumbly and ragged.

She looks him over, then looks at me with a concerned expression. She tries to speak but I interrupt her, "As well, tell the location manager that I'm done volunteering."

Her face pales, and her expression goes blank.

As I stumble away I feel more and more like a lemon being extracted by a juicer, I'm getting too weak for consciousness. I'm so tired, I can't stay awake. I feel my eyes closing uncontrollably when I try to keep them open, even adrenaline isn't helping me now. Slumber is sweeping me off my feet.

I stumble back the way I came, to see them one more time. I want them to understand what they've done. People are talking to me, asking me questions, but I can't make out what they're saying. I can feel their piercing gazes; some kids are even following me back. After a while, I see my shoes land on a white, polished surface; my crowd has dispersed and I'm finally alone with the biggest troubles in my life, ready to let them go.

As I doze off I hear a gasp of air. I don't have time to interpret it, I can't comprehend or understand anything. I look up and stare at the ceiling as I take a breath, darkness sweeping over my eyes. The sweet lullaby of comatose carries me away.

My vision is blurry as I wake up. I hear voices, but not clearly. They're screaming my name but it's as loud as a whisper until I fully come to. Victoria and Rose are hunched over me, their faces full of worry; Victoria seems hateful but I can smell the concern on her. As usual, their faces disgust me.

Sleeping isn't a good idea next to a visioneer like Rose. When we sleep we usually can't control what we think and we tend not to remember it anyway. Visioneers can read anybody's mind at all times; whatever I was thinking when I was asleep could have been true... Or it could be something I wasn't willing to admit. My home, my ambitions or lack thereof, my deepest, darkest secrets. A long bridge, an invisible rope tied around my waist, somebody pulling me across. I feel unsatisfied and afraid. Perhaps now she understands that.

The kids try to help me up but I refuse their offer and shamble to an upright position. The pain rushes to me. My chest feels like it's going to explode, I can't even collect myself while this ache engulfs me. I feel the sensation of being stabbed with warm needles. My breathing grows heavy as I try to calm down.

Over several minutes of panting and gasping, the pain subsides ever so slightly, but the anger doesn't at all.

I'm in a taxi. Traffic is … can reach you within, like, a couple days. I … believe it!

The voice continues in my head but they're diluted; somewhere miles away they're speaking to me. Around me are the walls of the training facility, in front of me are the kids. The thought occurs to me: this is my chance. I can find them. I take a deep breath as my dreams consume me. The thought of meeting another one is mesmerizing to me…

I'm ending this now. I'm done with these senseless heathens.

After resting for another several minutes, I finally stand up and brush myself off. An awkward silence fills the room, lingering like a terrible odor. I try to look them in the eyes, but both of the girls refuse my gaze. After what feels like years, Rose finally speaks up, "Mason…"

And with that, I blew up.

The moment I hear her voice, I can't control myself. This terrible demeanor and their appalling expressions, pretending like nothing even happened, *"No! Don't you try to call my name like nothing happened!"* Before I can even realize it, I'm screaming, "I'm so sick of you. All I ever do for you is *help* you! *Teach* you! *Train* you! Everything I've done was for *you!*" I stomp away from them, neither follow. "Months of this shit, months of having to deal with a bunch of *morons* like *you* and *this! This* is what I get." I try to calm down inhaling deeply, but my anger only worsens. I turn around with the most stern expression I've ever given. I look Rose dead in the eyes, "I believed in you, Rose." I pause to take a painfully deep breath, "I really did."

Examining the two, Victoria doesn't seem as confident anymore. Her bold expression has melted off and sorrow has drowned her. Rose, further back, is sobbing, trying to wipe away her grievances but tears keep streaming down her cheeks. Her beautiful golden hair has been tarnished, her dress is getting soaked. Her toes are locked towards each other; she's half way into being curled into a ball.

I can feel Rose's depression and anxiety in my head, but it doesn't faze me a single bit. Any other day, any other time I'd feel devastated, but I can't take it. I *tried* to feel bad for them. I'm over it.

I turn towards the exit. "Mason, *I'm sorry!*" I hear Rose shriek my name through her tears; I hesitate, but don't turn around. I confidently walk towards the exit directly in front of me. Rose's bawling grows louder and stronger, both behind me and in my head. I open the door to walk outside but before I can even take one step I'm accosted, I look down, dumbfounded as a pair of arms are wrapped tightly around me, embracing me, fastening my leather jacket tightly to my chest. I turn to see that it is Victoria resting her head on my back. I'm surprised, but I'm not getting deceived by this witch any longer.

I can hear her lightly weeping into my shoulder blade, stubbornly trying to hide her sadness. Her smug facade; this is the first time I've ever seen her without it. I put a hand on hers and force her off of me. Stumbling back, she looks at me in total astonishment as I glare back at her. I shake my head in disappointment.

Walking out, I slam the large metal doors behind me. This is it; I've decided here and now. I'm leaving and I'm never coming back.

I can't wait to see you! You know... I mean, it's probably pretty weird to say, but... it feels like ... forever. It almost feels ... born in the same ... separated at birth. Does that make sense? I mean ... anything about you, but it feels kinda ... you know? I doubt that makes sense. I'm sorry...

The voice continues bouncing around in my head; it's like the invisible rope they're tugging on is restricting my breathing at this point. Stress and anger well up in my chest, I feel like I want to explode but have no way to do so. I can feel the connection they describe, I feel what they're feeling... But have no way to respond.

They're not even talking to me, they're talking to each other.

Dread and fury expand in my heart. I can't feel anything but the utmost contempt for the entire world right now. I feel lost, like I have nowhere to go and I've just run away from home. I march along the empty road, away from the place I used to go every day. Without even looking back, I start my trek towards nowhere.

I feel numb in my arms, in my legs; I'm sure Rose figured it out. I'm too weak to use my powers, now. Even when I'm leaving, they're here to haunt me. My powers will painfully rejuvenate over time but it'll take quite a while. The thought only feeds the stress that's eating me alive. Even the ethereal voices are diluted; the invisible rope feels thinner.

As of right now, I'm the normal human I always wanted to be, walking into the sunset with no clear destination in mind. This is what I've always asked for…

Yet, I just want it to end.

CHAPTER III

WE AS ONE

Who are those voices in my head? In all honesty, I don't know. Ethereals have always had a connection that exists beyond reality, one that makes us feel and think as one. It's not something I've ever been able to explain; it's almost like we share ourselves, like we share a singular body. It's not a physical feeling, it's not something I can control or explain, it's just a sensation that ethereals have. Perhaps a sixth sense. If an ethereal is alive somewhere in this universe, I can perceive their presence. Sometimes they send me messages directly through my head.

There are three true ethereals; three pure-blooded.

One of the others is within the state, one on the way here. According to them, they're not even a day away. I know nothing of them, but I've woken up to conversations about meeting places and seeing each other for the first time ever. The first interaction of two ethereals I've ever heard of.

They're not half ethereals. Half-ethereals aren't as bonded with their ancestors, they're tainted with human blood. Half-ethereals don't have this speaking power; although they can listen. True ethereals have much stronger bonds with me, much tighter grips on their powers and other ethereals. The pull they give me is much richer, much more vivid than any others.

When they speak in my head, they don't speak through their voices, they speak through mine. They use my thoughts like an intercom speaker. Like a chat room with several people, but all of the messages are sent by me. I have an ever so subtle instinct to run towards them; sometimes I loathe the feeling. A constant sensation that I can't get rid of. I feel like a magnet being pulled in from afar but I'm up against a wall. I'm forced to deny my urges, to repel myself from the magnet that tries so hard to bring me in.

I plan to finally feed my instinct. Whatever this rope is, I'm getting entangled in it. For the first time, I shall give in to my desires. They've decided to meet on Rogue Street, a closed-down, abandoned street several miles South of me; a street I grew up on.

When I was young, Rogue Street wasn't closed down; in fact it was the heart of the city. Markets overran the entire street. Large businesses, small businesses; underground businesses even. The people there were always weird but friendly, even the authorities helped me when I was young and clueless. For being so lost, I never felt alone when I was walking that street.

It's finally time for me to make my way home.

My ethereal abilities are still depleted. Sitting and contemplating on the sidewalk for nearly an hour now, I'm realizing how long it's been since I've pushed myself like this. Really created a goal, really pursued something.

Without all of my natural ability, I won't be able to run like I used to. Getting from place to place is governed by reality now, I won't be able to get there by supernatural means. Rather, I will have to take... A taxi?

I can see... It must be...

The voices are quieter in my tired state. Like my mind is just as sore as my body and my thoughts aren't potent enough to communicate with.

Rogue Street is on the other side of the city, which means it's going to be too long of a walk. I've never really enjoyed the idea of public travel. In fact I've never even used it. My ability to run at high speeds for long amounts of time usually proves faster, I guess things will be a bit different this time.

Propping myself to my feet, I wait until I see a ride come by, but none do. The facility is pretty rural. In fact, *no* cars have come by. No people, either.

As I stand silently by myself, my head and chest begin to ache, my stomach starts turning. I'm used to pain but this feeling seems to be more than that. I pull out my phone; disgust quickly consumes me. Dragon Tech, a symbol of a silver European dragon embedded on the back, "A symbol of innovation for the public." The screen shimmers, the newest, most powerful technology available to the masses. I've always hated phones.

I've always hated the public.

I finally get a vehicle my way. The driver skids by quickly as he rolls down his window. His eyes are hard to look at. Purple, what I'm guessing are contacts, pierce through me like daggers. He glares at me as though I'm guilty of something; I can't help but feel uneasy around him. Something about him seems odd to me. Like a terrible odor, he sets me off; almost like he's not a real person. Hesitantly I get in the back seat, put my seatbelt on and look out the window as he drives away. The back seats are torn up, scratches relieve stuffing from the old fabric. A crack in the windshield becomes more and less visible as the sun vibrantly gleams on it.

The driver seems skittish, his eyes keep moving off the road to check on me in the rearview mirror. He looks young but his skin is loose and wrinkly around his eyes, it seems more due to stress than age. His hair falls down in a messy fashion hanging out of a newsboy hat, the tips frosted bright purple. His glasses are elliptical and thin, constantly sliding down his tiny nose in which he pushes them back up with his knuckle, usually giving the steering wheel a good tug as he does. He constantly turns the radio up then down, trying to get a volume somewhere between 12 and 14 but finding no success. He's very determined to get that radio to 13.

The emptiness of this long stretch begins to make me curious. I've never really taken this way so I wouldn't necessarily know, but it seems like there should be some more action than this.

His deep robust voice scares me out of my thought process. It almost had a rich melody to it, "It's odd to see you trying to pick up a ride on a closed street."

My eyes widen as I stare out the window. I think for a second. Are these roads closed? I guess I never would have known, it's so much faster for me to take my way through the forest to ever care about the way the road leads. Why the hell is it closed? Wonder begins to consume me. How many things about this facility don't I know? What kind of power do they have to close down a street... Or open a business on a closed street? Why are there no pedestrians? How did this driver get a car on a closed street, anyways?

"Mason, right?" He asks me staring through the mirror, "You know, it's bold of you."

I snap a glare a stern him, "What is? And how do you know my name?"

I instantly feel uneasy again as I look into his bright violet eyes. He looks back at the road and snickers, "Being out and about like this."

I open my mouth to speak, but I can't find the words. The rest of the ride is silent in the absence of my words. Something about him set every one of my gut feelings off; red flags were flying everywhere. This guy isn't one of your normal city weirdos. No, this guy was special.

Once miles of forest and foliage had passed us by, I finally realize why there's nobody here: the road is not only closed, but guarded as well. Around a bend, in the distance, I can see several armed guards patrolling large blockades, cutting all contact off from the city. I try to focus my vision with my bargain ability, but my abilities are totally exhausted. I can't budge it even a little.

Confusion begins to envelope me like thick rolling fog. Have I been so unobservant to not even know that somebody has miles upon miles of streets closed down?

Did this facility close down Rogue Street?

The guards quickly whip around, firearms raised and pointed at us. Before I can even ask, the driver whispers to me, "Gotta take a short cut." My eyes widen as I watch him tug the wheel into a sharp left turn; we go skidding directly into the forest. The squeal of the tires rubbing against the asphalt alerts the guards, but by the time they even have a chance to turn around, our vehicle has disappeared into the brush.

Gripping the seatbelt for my life, I begin to panic. This vehicle was never made to be anywhere but the road, if even that. A large trail leads deeper into the forest, tire marks make it obvious that somebody used a vehicle to create it. Every rock, stick, and bump expresses itself beneath the vehicle, bouncing and pushing the car around like a ping pong ball. Barely avoiding collisions, the driver keeps a firm grip on the wheel and an evil glare in his eyes, careening the car left and right to avoid obstacles.

I hear gunshots.

Behind me, I see bright flashes illuminate the forest path. Although I don't see any bullets flying, I can tell they're close by. Normally, a bullet wound wouldn't be lethal for me; my endurance can reach some pretty inhuman levels. Although, at the moment, a well-placed bullet could be lights out for me.

I feel a buzzing in my pocket. Again, this abominable company haunts my every move, every breath I take. I look out the window as trees and large trunks zoom by, getting closer and further as our wheels lose traction. From the understanding I have of the forest, we can't be inside for much longer. My breathing grows heavy and my heart pounds harder and harder. I can't even find the energy to speak.

The only thing that scares me more than bullets is a call from Theodore Drakone, owner of Dragon Technology Incorporated.

Drakone doesn't make personal contact with anybody. As an owner of a multi-billion dollar under-and-overground company, I'm sure he's very busy. I've only seen a picture of him during my orientation, and have never heard much about him, except for timid talk overheard in the hallways.

Lifting the phone and accepting the call, I put it to my ear, "This is-" My response is interrupted by a prominent bump beneath the wheel. I grunt as I try to compose myself.

"I'm glad I'm able to get a hold of you." I shudder. Drakone's voice is cold, his words cut deep into my ears as if they're being injected into my head, "We have an issue, Mr. Parker. I expect you to make your way back to the main building." He pauses for a brief moment, "You, of course, will be paid for your time."

I feel a dreadful shiver down my spine. "W-what do you mean, sir?" Another powerful bump almost sends the phone flying out of my hand. With barely enough time to hear his sentence, I grab the phone and place it against my ear again.

He grunts, "We will be checking employees for stolen equipment." He takes another pause. Enough time passes in between sentences for me to painfully grit my teeth. "I hope that isn't a problem… Mason."

Fear wraps itself around me, caressing me like death. I speak using all of my power and will to keep my composure, "N-no, sir.". With no response, no reply, I hear the phone beep as he hangs up on me. My hand trembles as I lower the phone; I drop it before I can put it back in my pocket. I can't stop shaking. It feels like he's watching me, it feels like he can still hear me when I speak. It feels like he left a hand and an eye on me, even while I can't hear him. As if he's right behind me.

Finally, one last bump, from curb-side to street, takes us back on a main road. A more rural side of the city; we're even getting close to my apartment. Nobody seems to be around to see us.

A swell of emotion fills my throat as I try to grab hold of the situation. From the kids to the ethereals to my work to this damned taxi driver; it's like my world is crashing down on itself. I don't understand what's happening, anxiety begins to well up inside me.

I can't avoid Drakone. This man not only has the power to take my job, but he has the resources and manpower to end my existence without even a trace, powers or not. I can't help but feel utterly intimidated by him, a feeling I'm not very used to. His words wrap around my brain like claws, like his commands are unavoidable, unforgettable.

Drakone has been deemed the most powerful man in the world. Many people would consider me blessed to work beneath him but nobody knows what's really going on, nobody understands his true intentions. Although, my true worries spawn from a single conversation. From his voice alone, this man emanates power. His commands have deep influence. It's as if parasites are crawling around beneath my skin.

I muster up enough courage to decide on a plan of action. I tap a finger on the taxi driver's shoulder, he tilts his head towards the mirror to look at me, his gross smile widening, "Yessir?"

"I'm sorry, but... I need to go somewhere else."

CHAPTER IV

DIRECTOR'S ORDERS

His request plays over and over in my head. Every single person of the branch is going to get a real good look at his face; he's hunting us down tonight.

The main building is a skyscraper. A beautiful, illuminating building in the thick of the city. Office workers, directors, manager; hundreds of totally normal employees work to market the legal aspect of the company. Testing out new tech, creating ideas, and marketing plans on new devices is what keeps this project funded.

Under the building are several rooms of laboratory equipment and engineering squads. Undercover scientists and doctors come at night to test new equipment and create new machines to help find signs of paranormal anomalies, non-humans using their power generally. People, like me and the kids, set off an aura of disturbance in the atmosphere much like a terribly pungent odor, one that usually only machines can see. This aura is what gives us away, what makes us terribly vulnerable to being caught. I, as a scout, leave in the morning equipped with a smuggled prototype machine called a scan breaker. These machines interrupt the signals that our company fires off, it keeps non-humans under cover. I've set two in the facility where the kids are hiding, one upstairs and the other below.

Drakone is on our ass, though. He's found out that somebody has been messing with their operations and he believes that's why we haven't been successful in our recent searches. It sounds like he plans on finding out who did it and he's not going to stop until he gets his way.

Something doesn't sit well with me, though. I've been with this company for nearly two years now; it's huge, the amount of surveillance they have is unfathomable. But even then, there's a couple scouts I've caught doing the same as me, for longer even. Yet, this is the first time I've heard of any suspicion.

What if this is where it all ends?

Situation, guys. The taxi I'm in just broke down ... has no idea how to fix it. He's trying ... making it worse.

Their voices quietly ring in my head.

After a couple of stops that make the brakes weep and some choice words from pedestrians, the driver finally parks along the sidewalk. Looking out the window I see my livelihood, the building I hate most in this world. It hurts to see it again, but the discomfort only worsens as I think that I'm not here for work this time. I'm here on my evening off because somebody wants to find me and wring my throat like a dish towel.

I reach into my back pocket and pull out my wallet, instantly noticing that my phone screen has been shattered from the impact of dropping it. Beneath the cracks of the black screen I see faint purple light glowing beneath it. I wish I understood what made technology work the way it does, this stuff is so foreign to me.

I try to gather and organize my thoughts. Within under half an hour, I've been through probably the thickest rough patch of my life. My anger for Rose has not eased yet, but rather has been sent to the back of my head, waiting for a better time to reach the surface. The invisible rope is almost unsensible at this point; whether it be the lack of power or too much on my mind, I can't really feel it. The shock from the drive has slowly melted away. I've seen terrible drivers before, I've just never been a passenger of one. Either way, we came out unscathed.

I open the door and step outside. I reach my hands in my coat pockets and have a mild to mid-range heart attack; I still have a scan breaker on me. It's small, smaller than my fist, I can fit it in my hand and close my fingers around it. I can't have this on me, it's one thing to have been caught smuggling equipment, it's another to show it off. I could try to put it back when I get in there but I have no idea what's going on in there, I don't know if I'll even get the chance to. I might get searched the moment I walk in. No, I need to dispose of it.

I look around for the best place to get rid of it, I doubt a simple trash can or dumpster will be good enough; the security and surveillance is much too strong for something that simple. It'd be too easy for them to find it again. Nervously, I turn to the sewers.

Abruptly, I shake my head. Near my feet is a sewer cap, a large metal plate that leads into a manhole; that'll be perfect. I've never truly known what's at the bottom of a sewer but I'm confident enough to believe they won't go digging through it.

I duck behind the vehicle as I try to remove the cap. I have trouble lifting the cover at first; suddenly it hits me how often my original powers come in handy, it's immensely heavier than I expected. Concentrating my strength, I lift an end just enough to throw the tiny device inside. The clinks and clanks it makes off the walls echo, followed by a distant *splash*.

My anxiety grows; the amount of effort it took to lift a simple manhole cover is actually scaring me. That's the kind of effort it should take me to lift the front end of a car. This is insane, the only time my physical lifting power should be this bad is if I'm exchanging it for something else.

I can barely recognize myself anymore.

As the driver skids off, the first thing I realize as I walk away is a very faint notification from my phone, a light yet angry beeping noise that slowly gets quieter and quieter. A notification for an anomaly nearby. I instantly begin to look around; where could there be a surreal using their powers? Wherever they are, I'm sure they're not safe here. I'm sure *I'm* not safe here. I don't see anything fishy going on around me.

Attempting to get out of my own head and ignoring the notification, I open the door to the front entrance. The lobby has a front desk with a single person; a pretty, young, unfamiliar lady. "Claire" is embedded in the steel name plate next to a vase filled with blooming roses. A sofa next to the entrance, lavender colored and pristine, is accompanied by a small table full of well-organized magazines, both untarnished from lack of use. The interior is well-kept and lightly colored, the light scent of strawberry-vanilla wafts through the air. I can't help but feel distressed and secluded from the idea that hell smells so good.

Walking up to the girl, I imagine some new line like, "Hi there, welcome to purgatory! You had an appointment this afternoon?" but she gives me the same line as usual.

"How can I help you today, sir?"

I take a deep breath, "Mason J. Parker, SCT-2173. Access to the basement, please."

She gives me a pretty smile as she types away on her computer. Her long brown hair shimmers in the sunlight through the clear glass doors behind me. I begin to realize the smell is coming from her; to be honest, the scent is calming.

"Identification, please?"

I roll up the right sleeve of my leather jacket revealing a Dragon Tech logo tattooed in silver beneath my wrist. She nods her head and clicks a button on her computer, "Right this way, sir!"

"Thanks," I reply insincerely.

An elevator behind the desk opens with an unsatisfying *ding*. I slowly march my way inside it, turning around to watch the door shut. Eerily, the elevator rumbles it's way down. What was a couple seconds felt like a year inside my little box. Slowly, the elevator drifts deeper and deeper.

I ... can you even ... just me?

What happens to the people taken in? What happens when Drakone captures somebody? When we bring them in, where do they go? Thoughts begin to swarm around in my head as I think about this. At first, I believed they just got killed... But there's no rhyme nor reason to it. I can't imagine a grudge match between one man and an entire species becoming this expensive.

Ding. The gateway opens again.

I hear the mechanisms in the entrance unlock. I walk past the steel hatch in front of me as it swings open in front of the sliding elevator doors. This reveals a short hall, leading only to another door merely six feet ahead. Unlike the front of the door which looks wooden and decorative, the back is made of reinforced titanium, equipped with 14 different types of automated locks. A code block and a fingerprint scanner allow me through. Casually, I take a step inside.

It shuts behind me, the mechanisms all beginning to function, squeezing themselves into the lock holes, cranking their way back into place. A final gear rotates in the center of the door driving a huge metal beam into the side of the wall locking it completely. I'm not getting out until Drakone gets what he wants.

I see two men lined up shoulder to shoulder with shy, nervous faces. After a moment to look around, the place is extremely quiet today. No bustling, no odors of labor, nothing. Minutes after lining up with the others, I hear the locks begin to unlock again. Two more men walk through with the same terrified expression. They line up with us, just as scared, just as stiff.

I look down the line of people. It's not hard to tell our jobs apart. Underground engineers tend to come uniformed in nice, dressy clothes. Suits, dress shirts, ties, nice leather shoes, things like that. The scientists and doctors wear normal clothes, khakis, jeans, shorts and t-shirts sometimes, coated with a long branded lab jacket that reaches their ankles. Most of them also have a custom-fit pair of goggles made by the company snapped on their forehead. Scouts, like me, wear seemingly normal clothes, but we all have the same in common: Long pants, tennis shoes, a white t-shirt issued by the company, and a long sleeve jacket. As long as our outfits fit those guidelines, we're free to wear whatever we want.

Dozens of people stream into the line, which is slowly becoming a mob, over the course of the next ten minutes or so, nobody taking any time to chat. The tension grows as more people join, an awkward silence hangs around the room like a mammoth is hogging most of the breathing space.

The tension is strongest after our final attendant, a short redheaded scout, adheres to the line. Her bright red shiny hair reaches just past her shoulders, her jean jacket seems brand new. Her company t-shirt, on the other hand, is drenched in sweat.

The room we're in is a huge 50 foot by 50 foot space with concrete walls and a steel balcony about ten feet up. Doors lead into engineering spaces, science labs, and whatever else is needed to pull of the stunts this company does.

The balcony is scattered with different machinery parts, seemingly popular prototypes. Some devices I can't really make out, mostly just scattered bits of wires and scrap metal. Although, I can make out large black robotic body parts. An arm, portions of a leg scattered around, each limb larger than me. My brow furrows at the sight. A drop of sweat beads down my forehead.

As I investigate the area with my eyes, a large gleaming… No, a *huge* gleaming device catches my attention. Suddenly, it's a little harder to breathe. The corner of a wall upstairs blocks most of my view, but past the edge I peak over at a giant mechanical construction at least several yards tall. Humanoid in shape, I see it's glinting darkly-colored metal limbs posed menacingly. Its gigantic feet aren't touching the ground, rather large steel rods suspend it in the air from the ceiling. The colossal machine brings dread through my body, my stomach sinks.

When did we get one of those?

One of the doors on the north wall slides open. Out stride two men dressed in nearly identical suits; dark charcoal blazers and matching slacks with a white undershirt and grey ties with a gleaming silver logo. The only difference between the two is that one of their suits has a silver trim around the edges. Their composure is neat and formal, their faces are both stern and chilling.

The one with no lining, an older man with thinning grey hair and a rugged face, is our branch supervisor. Frankly, I'm not sure what his name is since we usually just refer to him as supervisor. His current acquaintance, though, is none other than the dreaded Theodore Drakone. Just like the pictures, lifeless eyes and a rich man's composure.

A lot shorter than I expected, honestly.

Drakone walks in front followed closely by his henchman. His silver-trimmed suit shines, the bright lights above emphasizing his dead green eyes. His skin is deeply tanned and well kept but his body is scrawny like there's sticks beneath his suit. His hair is dark and short, immaculately kept with a single streak of grey towards the center of his forehead. A well-kept, shortly trimmed beard reaches down his jawline, white blending into the edges.

Every step he takes echoes in the eerily silent room. All of us stand straight as husks, empty beings filled with nothing but terror. Petrified, we watch them close in with only our gaze.

The man behind him is far less attractive. His diminishing hair is light and barely existent, only a small number of thin hairs still prevail to create his ugly comb-over. His face is shaven and wrinkled, dark circles linger beneath his eyes. His irises are colored a dark shade of grey, quite similarly to mine. The biggest difference, though, is the emptiness. His eyes seem hollow, fitting of the way he walks. He composes himself sternly but empty, raw motions and mechanical actions. It's as if he's a robot being piloted by someone else.

Both of them have their hands folded behind their backs. It's as if they've choreographed this, they're in sync. Drakone wastes no time, as he slowly advances towards us he speaks, "Samuel, pat them down," his voice echoes in the large building; his accent is faint and his voice is deep. Halting, Darkone looks around at everybody, then looks me directly in the eye.

And for that moment, I didn't even have enough courage to blink.

His beaming glare punctures right through me. As if I was stuck between several blades and a wall, I feel a sharp pain in my head and my heart. My ears begin to ring. His glare is a guillotine, I can feel my neck against the wooden brace. Anxiety fills my body replacing my blood with lava. I begin to sweat at the sight of him; never have I been so terrified of a single man before.

"Yes, sir," the accessory says as he walks towards the mob. He brings his hands out and begins thoroughly patting down everybody in the room, one by one. I'm drenched in sweat, Drakone's eyes haven't left me for even a second, not even a blink.

What must have been a single silent minute became the longest session of torture I've ever endured. The only time Drakone broke eye contact with me was when my supervisor got between us. As he pats me down I shiver. Down my arms, my sides, my legs. Handling my back and my chest, he even reached around my neck and face. His hands were rough and scarred, oddly familiar to me. He smelled like cheap cologne and oil. The weirdest thing, though, was that this man's presence was… Somehow comforting.

Without a word, he strides away from me. The evil being was finally looking somewhere else, following Samuel with his ugly grimace. It took this long to realize that I've been holding my breath this whole time. Quietly gasping, air fills my lungs and drowns out some of my horror.

I attempt to compose myself once again but I'm interrupted by a loud *clunk*. Looking behind me, I see everybody has made room to watch a small device roll across the floor. In the center of the pit is a bewildered young man with glasses and neat, stylish clothing. Samuel watches the device roll its way across the solid ground until it's stomped on and destroyed by the big man himself.

Staring directly at the young engineer, Drakone smiles.

It looks like the taxi isn't … guess I'm on foot. But … won't give up … find you guys.

The room has no people here, for everyone is made of lead and fear. Useless stone statues. Never have I felt more human than now, the moment I was most vulnerable.

Silence continues to fill the room. The boy, in one swift motion, runs back while dragging a hand on the ground. A sonic boom is released from his fingertips as the concrete begins to wave like rope.

Several employees fly back in its wake but none of them take the blunt force more than Drakone.

The anomaly notification on my phone goes absolutely haywire.

The boss flies back, tumbling a few times before summersaulting backwards to an agile stance, his feet spread apart and one hand on the ground. He lifts his head with an angered expression, blood dripping from his lips.

The balls on this boy could make a grown man cry.

Are you ... I can feel your distress.

The voice goes off in my head and I'm instantly astonished. I can feel it, too, massive amounts of distress. I didn't even know ethereals could share emotion.

I'm very distressed. What must be the second voice peers in my head as the distress begins to grow. Drakone grabs Samuel's attention only to nod at him, confirming his next action. With extremely fast reflexes his puppet-man pulls a pistol from his jacket pocket. The boy is already at the door waiting for its opening but it's taking much more time than he has. Samuel fires.

Suddenly motionless, the boy topples over. Blood begins pouring from his left shoulder blade. The loud percussion of the firearm, his body hitting the ground, and his blood-spattered glasses flying across the room reverberate against my ears.

After a short break to breathe, Samuel wanders forward and picks up the body, throwing it over his shoulder as he follows the leader towards the north wall. Blood begins to stain his suit. His expression didn't change once the entire time. I puke in my mouth but cover it with my hands, unable to hold back my absolute disgust. Unfathomably revolted, I feel tears streaming uncontrollably down my cheeks.

Even worse, though, I feel something stronger than disgust. A tugging, I feel magnetized towards them as they walk away holding the boy's limp body. Like I'm chained up, being pulled away from my spot on Earth, I realize there's an ethereal in the room.

The invisible rope is pulling me towards the big man himself.

CHAPTER V

THE REASON WE STRUGGLE

I've never known happiness like I did when I struggled the most. Growing up as a kid on the streets really hardened me, made me learn how to fend for myself. I never had hobbies or went out, money is too sparse for that kind of play. Or it *was*, at least.

When I was an infant, before I could even walk, I was sent to a small foster home in California. Never aware of my parents, afraid of my powers and treated like shit, I ran away at the age of 13, heading as far north as my legs could take me.

I met too many people in the city; criminals, businessmen, every color of personality, every color of hair. Most were nice but none were sincere. They all wanted something from you, a piece of you. There's only one person who ever treated me like a real person.

An old homeless man took me under his wing when I was young, treated me like his son when I was alone and hungry. Even though he didn't have a job, he knew how to have fun with what he had. Begging on the streets brought a lot of criticism and hate; every time I saw someone sputter rude comments towards him my temper would surpass its limits but he wouldn't let me do anything about it. He stayed calm and collected, his head was always level. I had to learn that from him to survive. "Some battles aren't meant to be won," he'd tell me.

His name was Robert, but I called him Red.

I never understood it. How did he stay so cool? How was he so happy when he had the worst cut from society? Begging brought in a livable amount of money for us but not a whole lot. Even so, Red decided to share his minimal fortunes with me and take me out to do fun things whenever we got the chance. I couldn't even begin to thank the stranger I met on the streets for helping me through my life, I wish I still had the chance to.

But through the years, life got rough and money became scarce. When I was 15 I turned to fighting. Downtown, there's an underground fight club that pays pretty well if you're good at it. At such an age, I became the youngest underground champion fighter. Nobody knew that I was using my powers to aid my fighting, they only knew that I was young and I was winning. Rising through the ranks, fighting began to bring in more and more money but the truth was that I absolutely hated it and Red knew it.

"I can see the life leaving your eyes, boy. This ain't right for you, is it?" he spoke lightly upon my deaf ears. It brought in money that we could use to have fun together, to do things together. He deserved it; he deserved the rewards I reaped from others, it was the only way I could pay him back for what he did. He tried so many times to stop me but never once did I.

But we didn't have fun with the money. At this point, we stopped having fun at all.

I became lost in my new profession. Life was no longer about enjoyment or thriving, it became about grinding, fighting, and surviving. My primal urges got the best of me, I got greedy and hostile towards everybody. I regretfully grew into it, becoming more willing to fight, getting better at fighting. With my newfound skills, I turned to violence to solve my problems. Red knew every step of the way that he was losing me to a monster within myself. I didn't listen, I didn't stop.

I wish I realized what he was trying to explain to me before. It's not about surviving, but making the best of the small things we have. "To look at somebody else with envy is to disrespect the little things, boy." He always seemed so wise when he explained it to me, "If we get tangled up in the if's, and's, or but's of life, we find no time for the roses and pretty skies. And if we can't watch the sky, what's the point of living on the surface, huh boy?"

Red was wise… But Red is dead.

He's dead because I was too ignorant and too stubborn to listen. It's a fear of mine that he knew the whole time that losing him would be the only way I'd wake up from my nightmares.

The thoughts mesmerize around in my head over a pain-staking hour of searching. After a satisfied grunt from Drakone, we are released. We all flood out with urgency.

Every step I take is swallowed by the trampling steps of the horde I'm in; the tight space is beginning to make me claustrophobic. So many people all clumped together is making my head spin.

I look back at the building as I walk out, every person leaving is totally speechless. Cars drive away, zooming past me as I stand, hopeless and quiet.

My mind is foggy and my brain is in pieces. I can't even begin to comprehend what's going on so instead I just choke on it. I look down and stare at the concrete beneath my feet, glaring at my shoes until everybody leaves, until I'm completely alone again. For the millionth time, I'm alone.

Interrupting my wallowing, a small kitten approaches at my toes. Startled, I jump back and lose my balance, falling backwards. The kitten's coat is dirty and tarnished, its fur different shades of grey. As it brushes up against my body its vibrant purple eyes take me by surprise. Piercing me with its intense line of sight, it cuddles against my side and underneath my hands.

I've never seen a kitten with purple eyes, how odd.

It has a very intense glare, I find an eerie sensation from it. Although, in contrast, this baby cat seems to be a little more gentle and careful. I've never been one for animals but this time is a little different. As it brushes past me, my breathing slows down and my conscience starts to soothe.

Death scares me. Not dying, but the death of the innocent. I've only witnessed it a handful of times, and each time I lost it; Red's death was the last wire that snapped in my head. I wasn't able to control myself when I watched it all go down, it's like somebody grabbing my chest and chaining me down. The feeling is so intense, somehow so painful. It fills my eyes with nothing but anger and fear; it makes me want to kill.

Red's murderer was the second person I ever killed; his face will never leave my mind. His fear, his surprise, his face, the way his eyes begged for mercy. I can never forget the person I've become because this person won't get out of my head. This monster, this demon, this murderer inside me. It feels like he's made a cozy little nest inside my heart; his presence slowly turning my blood black.

Before Red died, he told me that there were going to be a lot of things I'd see that I wouldn't be prepared for. He told me that the world is bigger than me but I still walk on it; that I shouldn't let it walk on me. "It doesn't matter what the world throws at you, boy, you get back up and keep running. The only one who can stop you is you," he'd put his arm around me and watch the sunset over the bridge when he talked with me like this. "Even after I'm gone. When it's all eyes on the main man here," he'd point at me and chuckle, the pride potent in his voice, "you need to learn how to stand tall." He looked directly into my young eyes when he said it, "I believe in you, Mason."

Over many minutes and miles of mental hurdles, my courage builds with my new purple-eyed companion. I try to drive my fears and anxiety away with some success. The thought of that young engineer's life being taken is haunting me, but there's no longer anything I can do. I've heard of many getting killed, people and surreals alike, but seeing it is so much worse.

Although it slightly perturbs me, I pet the kitten. Her company settles my nerves, gets my mind off the bad stuff. I'm reminded that I have a goal and I plan to do something about it. I can't keep letting things get in my way; not kids, not work, not even death shall stop me.

With my newfound courage and my new baby friend, I begin my way towards Rogue Street. The thoughts begin to flock inside my head as I think about it, maybe Drakone is an ethereal. Although, if that's true then the boss would be the quiet one talking in my head with the other. Why would the leader of a group that kills ethereals *be* an ethereal? What kind of hypocrisy is that?

What if he plans on killing the other when they meet?

Without me even noticing, my walk has turned into a light run. I can feel myself getting exasperated much faster than usual; my powers are gone, I can't bargain my stamina. My breathing gets heavier even when I try to fight it but I don't have time to get tired. I need to beat Drakone there, I *have* to.

I don't think I can ... by today, I'll ... rest. I've got enough ... for the night, I think there's a couple...

The words ring in my head scattered around with my other thoughts. As if there are rubber balls bouncing around in my skull, my head hurts so bad it's pounding. My mental exhaustion is almost outperforming my physical exhaustion.

Goodnight, I hope to see you soon.

I look at my broken phone for the time; it's about seven o'clock at night. I try to focus on what's happening from their side; find anything, feel anything, see anything I can from them. Their distress, their joy, their presence. I may not know them, but I've always *known* them.

Although, the harder I try, the more hopeless it seems.

I'm not running anymore; I'm walking so slow I might as well have stopped. If they're taking a night to rest, I've got a night to rest. Looking around me, I see that the deeper into the city I go, the denser the population gets. People bustle by me, bumping my shoulder and pushing me around. Angry, I slip into an alleyway where I can get out of the path of the public.

The large alley I creep into is dark in comparison to the evening sky, the massive buildings beside me block most of the incoming light. Around me are puddles, drips of dirty water splatting down from above. I see more and more insects crawling on the walls as I inch closer to the end of the path. The smell here is intense, like rotting food. A dumpster is hidden behind a notch in the wall next to me, barely locked shut against the heaping pile of trash pushing it open. Disgusted but too tired to fret, I sit down with my back against the corner right next to the garbage. My nose in anguish and my head tilted, the kitty takes shelter in the crook of my neck.

After resting for a minute and regaining my composure, I notice the smell of burning. The sound of a faint dripping barely surfaces against the footsteps and chatter outside but there's no signs of fire. Feably, I get up and investigating around the alley towards the street, loud crackles resonate behind me. Looking back I see nothing. Across the street far in front of me, glass windows compliment brightly colored signs and big rooms full of families and couples eating out, yet none of the signs are sparking, nothing seems to be burning.

My phone begins to beep, slowly escalating.

A flash bursts behind me, it's light so intense it becomes overwhelming. I look back again, there's a smog rising from the concrete, billowing like smoke. The kitten jumps up and burrows into my jacket, its body just small enough to fit. I put a hand on it protectively as I slowly advance towards the cacophony.

The blinding flash radiates again, so intense that I'm forced to shield my eyes. As the light slowly decays, it forms into a tall, scrawny male. A tattered, dirty white button up shirt stained in blood around the shoulder. His pale skin has light scratches that have begun to scab over. His dressy brown shoes have lost all their luster, a pair of broken glasses are barely hanging onto his face by the tips of his tiny ears. He's hunched over his knees and panting, gripping his shoulder where the blood seems to drain from.

It's the engineer from work.

I gasp and my eyes illuminate. Creepily, his gaze lights up with hope the moment he sees me. Quickly, he runs up and grabs my arm, I don't even have the time to react before he latches onto me with an alligator's grip. The moment his hand touches me, I hear a static noise from my back pocket as the beeping comes to a halt. I don't have my powers right now, I can't do anything to defend myself. Not against somebody like him.

Zap!

My vision goes stark white for the quickest second I've ever been able to comprehend; suddenly, I don't know where I am.

It's darker due to a raised canopy, I can hear water dripping from somewhere above, a little harsher than the droplets in the original alley. We're in the corner of another roofed, skinny alley; so deep that I can't even see the street. My head begins spinning in confusion. The boy is poised and leaned up against the stone surface, peeking around the wall's corner.

My body feels tingly, I have trouble controlling my limbs. I feel my knees trying to buckle on me. I try to bargain my stamina for the strength in my legs but my efforts are obviously void. It's a habit, I guess, even when I don't have the option.

I crinkle to the ground like I'm made of empty parts, I do my best to support myself with my arm but my elbows fail under the pressure. Folding like paper, I wait for the feeling in my arms and legs to slowly come back. My vision is watery and blurry, I don't have enough sensation to make out any of the fine details of my surroundings.

My eyes widen as I watch a small, limp kitten tumble down my body from inside my jacket. I panic, but there's no fruits to my efforts.

"I'm sorry Mason, I-I know you're s-struggling right now but I don't have time, please just… Just, uh, listen," he says with his hands up in a stuttery panic as he forges towards me. I look up as well as I can. Little by little, starting with my toes and fingertips, I try to gain control of my body again. As the tingling goes away, I slowly work myself into an upright position, but an attempt to stand higher forces me against the wall. I'm sitting now, hunched up over my knees, my breathing getting heavier. Looking over to the small, limp kitten, it seems to be suffering the same. Unable to move, panting, and utterly terrified.

Just like me, she's totally helpless.

I take a good look at the boy's face. Tears are streaming down his cheeks and dried blood is staining most of his clothes and skin. Although, through the dying shimmer in his broken glasses, I see him mustering his courage. I can see the hysteria in his eyes.

Why do I always get dragged into shit like this?

CHAPTER VI

WHEN THE LIGHTS IN HIS EYES EXTINGUISH

I can't even begin to understand what's going, I can't think of the first question to ask. Why are we here? *How* are we here? His breathing gets heavier as he looks subtly from side to side. He whispers to me, "We can't stay anywhere for too long. T-they're going to find us."

I open my mouth to speak but before I can he crouches down, resting a light hand on my shoulder. His gentle touch feels soothing to my useless limbs but the sweet feelings are interrupted by another burst of light. My vision blurs totally white again, I can't see anything for less than a mere moment. It doesn't hurt, but I'm not comfortable in any way. I try regaining myself but I can't move. I can't tell what position my body is in; it feels like we're moving forward but that may just be the world crumbling around me, not totally sure.

There's a window to my right side, trees and clouds are flying by us. Moving just my eyes I try to soak in the blurry details; next to me towards the aisle sits the boy, his elbows resting on his legs as he hunches over, staring at his once-nice shoes. The fabric I'm sitting on seems speckled blue but dirty and stained yellow, torn in several spots. My arms are slouched on the side rests, my head falling uncontrollably sideways. He props my head up with his hand and lies me back but my body is trying to slither out. In front of me are seats similar to my own; it seems that I'm on a bus.

"Mason, d-don't leave just yet," he whispers to me as he stares out at the moving scenery, now upright and formal. His words resonate within me, he sounds like one of the kids. If I had time or energy, I'd be angry. But I don't.

I look to him, my strength draining from my body. I'm seeping over like an ooze in a sitting position; the engineer puts a hand on my chest and props me back up against the seat. With the best condescending look I can muster, I attempt to look at him, "Dude, what are my options?"

He takes a good look at me and bites his lip. His leg is bouncing up and down frantically, I can see a drip bead off his forehead from his short messy hair, his hair gel getting ruined by the sweat. He looks at me. The sun is hitting his glasses hard enough for me to see my sideways reflection in the spiderweb crack. He whispers to me as he looks away again, "They know you're an ethereal, Mason." My eyes widen as I try to freak out but my body responds by oozing over even faster.

"Make it so I can move again so I can slap some sense into you!" I angrily whisper to him, "Don't say shit like that out loud!"

The jello that has foretaken my body doesn't stand a chance anymore, this time I'm moving. Although, what felt like coordinated movement translated to light jiggling but any response is better than nothing. I panic, "What the hell do you mean by that?" I cry out, struggling like a handcuffed ball of playdough, "I do *not* care what you want from me!"

I'm not whispering anymore, I'm actually yelling now. There's nobody directly next to us but the people across the bus are staring. I've lost the ability to care. He calmly props me up again, leaning me back against the seat. I'm starting to regain my body just a little bit more. Holding his hand against my chest to keep me up he says, "Calm down, Mason. Now isn't the time."

I furrow my brows at his words. I'm furious now, stunned by the idea that he has the nerve to tell me to calm down. I open my mouth ready to make a bigger scene but he interrupts me, "Stay focused. I need your help right now." As he says this, he peaks around the seat behind him while the bus comes to a slow and subtle stop. Watching the entrance I see two armored guards similar to the ones at the barricades by the facility march onto the bus. "They're onto us, Mason," he says without even taking a glimpse at them.

This boy must be a magnus… But I've never seen anybody use whatever witchcraft he's conjuring up. Whatever it is, I hate it. I want my damn body back.

He looks at me with sorrow and determination, "I'm sorry, Mason, but this is for both of us." I glare back at him. His hand on my chest becomes much firmer as he inhales deeply.

What the hell do you mean by *us*?

I will never get used to electricity and I will never feel anything other than burning hatred for it. I'm laying in a well made bed right now, soft sheets cushioning my weight as my body lies completely limp. My body isn't just resisting my actions this time, I literally can't move.

The boy is walking along the side of the bed, pacing back and forth. I don't understand how he's still able to move. I try to open my mouth but I don't have enough control. Instead, my lips begin to droop slightly over my cheeks as my words sputter out as mumbly garbage. Whatever confidence and elegance he had at one point has melted away. He rambles as he trots, "Look, Mason, I know this is a lot to take in at once but you have to *please* listen to me."

I roll my eyes, it's not like I have a choice. The anger bubbles within me but my helplessness helps it evaporate away. He continues, "Right now Drakone and his lackeys are following me. Every time I zap from place to place I leave a huge trail for them to sniff out," he looks at me. "Don't worry, you'll regain your muscle movement soon enough."

Not soon enough.

"You need to help me get out of their hair, Mason. Please." He stops in his tracks looking directly at me with the most intense glare I've seen a boy give me, "They were going to go for you, first."

My heart jumps into my throat. I had a feeling for so long but I never expected it; they've known for a while, I bet. What, did they find me too valuable to kill just yet? I bet they were waiting for a good opening.

He interrupts my thought process, "Being at that company is the only way I can know that my brother is safe, that my brother hasn't been caught yet."

Over the course of the next ten minutes or so, my body somberly begins to return to me as I try to stand. My knee begins the buckling process but I catch myself by grabbing the bedpost just in time. I take a deep breath and sit down on the bed next to the magnus, I see a tear creeping down his cheek. Quietly, I claim, "You owe me answers." He glances over at me. I take a deep breath. With a final regain of my physical power, I ask him, "What was that power you just used? How did we get here? *Where* is here? And who's your brother? Why did you pick me for this shit?" I pause to think for a second, then continue, "How did you know I was an ethereal? *Who the hell are you?*" My voice gains volume as I work myself up.

He chuckles a little bit, it almost sounds like he's choking. I want to consider it cynical but I know it's not. He glances back down, "It's called *jumping*. I tried to teach it to my brother years ago, but it's no easy task," he looks down at his hand as electricity begins climbing his arm. Once it reaches his fingertips it dissipates, a new ring of energy spawns higher up his forearm. "'Turning a body into energy, such as light or sound, so they can move at unparalleled speeds through obstacles,' that's how it was explained to me." The electricity stops as he furiously grabs his glasses and throws them across the room, shattering completely. "Your body has never experienced that kind of transportation. Ripping through the atmosphere, your atoms separated to get through the walls we passed. For somebody who's never done that before, you took it pretty well," his voice calms down as he explains.

This kid had a whopping one conversation with me before ripping my body up atom from atom and sent me flying through walls and vehicles at mach levels of speed. I may not have enjoyed our time together, but I have to respect this dude's fortitude.

"I'm not totally sure where we are. I can't see very well when we're traveling that fast, so I'm really shooting in the dark. Moving vehicles and underground rooms are good at resisting tracking, but I never know where I am in great detail." He stares down for a second, then scratches his head as if he's trying to recall all of my questions, "There's a surprising amount of empowered at our company. Company keeps them alive because more often than not, they're useful to them."

I shake my head. I knew it.

He continues, "I have a hunch that the boss is one, too. Can't prove it but I bet he is." I shiver a bit, I was right about that, too. Theodore is an ethereal and he's hunting the other ethereal down. Maybe he plans to employ them; probably against their will, if anything. Maybe he just wanted us in the same room.

With a pause he grabs a handful of sheets and squeezes them, "As for my brother," a tear crawls down his bloody face, "his name is Logan."

CHAPTER VII
A HOP, SKIP, AND ZAP AWAY

"Hold on, Mason," he chokes up as he grabs my arm. My vision transitions from white to a new setting in mere milliseconds. The new place is cold but humid. The walls and floor are made of solid stone, the only entrance I see is a couple-foot or so tall crawl space entrance on the opposite wall. I stumble over towards a corner behind me keeping myself leaned against it. The boy is propped up against the adjacent wall. His arms are crossed, he's anxiously tapping his foot, each tap echoing in the silence. Lit with a single dying light bulb, I can't even fully see the other corners where the dark walls meet.

I can't believe it. This is the big brother that Logan has never talked about. It makes sense, this guy seems like he'd take a bulldozing standing up. If anybody was going to shelter the kid it would be him. His build is pretty similar to Logan's but more toned, his jaw is sharper and his face is obviously more matured. Other than that and the foot of difference in height, they're basically identical.

I'm beginning to realize that, avoidable or not, I've got a lot of problems piling up on my plate right now. Frankly, this dude seems to be my best bet at survival now; I gather some strength and mutter, "What's your name?"

He takes a deep sigh before extending his arm and open hand out towards me, "Jayden, third rank engineer." His voice has become sturdy and his expression has steeled. His courage fulfills his voice as his eyes get a little brighter with determination.

I nod my head; my legs are still struggling but I muster myself enough to reach his hand and shake. I've never been a fan of formal introductions but it'd feel wrong to ignore him, "Mason, second rank scout."

With a quiet yet manly sniffle, Jayden wipes away his tears. He turns his back to me and begins to pace away. I watch the darkness cover him like a blanket, his words growing cold, "Help me take Dragon Tech down, Mason."

A magnus doesn't control electricity, they control energy. The wavelengths of sound, the light that shimmers around us, the things we feel but can't see. Jayden showed me a feat of power I've only heard of when he sent us spiraling through several feet of dirt, soil, and stone, into a concrete box who-knows-how-many feet below the ground. I can't believe that this whole time Logan had this ability waiting to be used, yet he still can't use his taser hands right.

Logan didn't live with parents or guardians, he lived with his brother. "We both moved into the facility together, I was 7 at the time, when our powers became apparent. Grandma decided it was best to give us over to those who knew how to deal with a situation like this," he says with some pain in his voice. He shakes his head, "Not like she took care of us, anyways."

I see why Logan wants to be a hero now, he's got one hell of a role model to live up to. The whole time Jayden has been there to protect him from a life that he can't comprehend. When Jayden left, Logan tried to take his place but he was pathetically unsuccessful. He longs to be like the brother that took care of him when nobody else would. He wants to be a man that can step up and face the challenges of life but his flesh is almost as soft as his bitter heart.

It seems that Jayden has gotten into a lot more conflict than Logan ever has, having better than full control over his abilities. Logan's been watched and sheltered his whole life, even when Jayden was kicked out he kept watching from afar. He never stopped making sure that Logan was okay, even when he wasn't there, even though Logan doesn't know he is.

But Jayden was born alone.

I examine the pain and tension in his eyes as the gears in his brain start cranking. He may be brave but he's also in over his head. I'm not sure if it's his brother pushing him towards this or something from a while back; either way, there's a fire in his eyes.

Jayden's plan to take down the company sounded pretty outrageous when the words first hit me, but I want to believe that it's possible.

My thoughts translate into rambles as I talk Jayden's ear off about my past couple of weeks. I tell him about the kids at the facility, while not including Logan's name, and my time as a scout while I was there. I tell him about the voices I hear in my head, the fact that there is somebody out there waiting to meet our director, somebody out there who believes that they're going to meet someone they were destined to accommodate. I explain to him that our director plans on killing them, on taking advantage of their trust and dismantling them. I tell him how I listen to these voices in my head, helplessly, with no idea on how to respond back. I can't warn them. Even if I could, everybody would hear it. Theodore included.

"I wish I knew how to clarify how I use my power," he says to me in a quiet, collected tone. "I wish I could teach somebody else how I do what I do. I don't know, it just kinda happens at this point, I guess. I have no idea how to explain it."

His words bounce through my skull like a ball, repeating over and over in my head.

It feels like I'm crippled, as if everybody else was born with a natural ability I don't have. It's shameful knowing that out of three in existence, I'm the one I'd deem most useless. Not even explanation would grant me the ability.

"I want to save them," I say. My voice is quiet and weak, I'm trying to put strength in my tone but I sound like a coward, "I want to be in that meeting spot before anybody else gets there. I want to be able to save them from what's going to happen."

I look down at a small puddle accumulating at my feet. It's funny, I can't even recognize myself. What have I been doing for so long? It's so hard to remember who I've become.

Jayden looks around somberly until something hits him. I watch his jaw drop ever so slightly as his muscles tense up. He raises a fist to his lips and begins to chew on his thumbnail, contemplating. He slowly ascends off the bed and starts walking around, pacing back and forth relentlessly. Silence fills the room. His focus is immense, he reminds me of a version of Logan with poise. He's like what I used to plan for Logan to be one day.

He suddenly halts. Lifting his hand from his lips, he points a finger up, "I have an idea."

Jayden begins to explain to me as he crafts his master plot. His plans fall together like puzzle pieces, his strategy is cunning. As he explains it to me, I can see the plan unfolding in my head as it happens. I can almost see it, I can feel every footstep I take as he elaborates it for me. My thoughts on his ideas bump around my brain, changing and transforming as I hear him speak.

My eyelids grow heavy as I process the information. His voice begins to lull me to sleep, his voice grows quieter as my body falls on the bed and my energy depletes completely.

When I wake up I'm sitting. We've moved somewhere else; Jayden is still next to me but he's wide awake, he probably was for a while. I watch him as he stares longingly out the window, trees and plant life pass by us at high speeds, colors whirl around outside as the sun begins to peak. This isn't a bus, I can hear the tracks streak against the wheels of the locomotive ahead of us.

I'm on my way guys, I'll be there soon.

Normally, a plan of this magnitude needs rehearsal, it needs time, it needs expertise and skill. We don't have those things. Though, of course, Red wouldn't be very proud if I didn't make due with what

I've got. He always knew how to make the best of only what you had, and I'm not planning on letting him down today.

Slowing down within a skinny tunnel, I watch as the walls outside the window begin to stop racing past us. The designs and graffiti on the wall are visible now, we come to a complete stop. With Jayden and I sitting in the very back, we watch as people drain out and pile in, people squishing together to make enough room to sit. I've never been a huge fan of trains, they always seem so cramped and hard to fit into, so impractical.

A loud ding goes off rattling in my ears. I look up, the conductor speaks out the words as they scroll across the screen above us, "Next stop: Rogue Street Station!"

CHAPTER VIII

WHEN A PLAN FALLS APART

'm scared, my heart is racing. Sweat is dripping down my forehead. I can feel my powers slowly coming back to me, not at normal pace; my powers are almost completely refreshed, I can feel myself almost completely back to my normal ethereal self. Jayden's plan to refresh myself harmlessly, it's the fastest way for me to get my power back without hurting anybody.

The hardest part about using my power is consent. Draining somebody of their soul or giving somebody a piece of mine isn't just under my authority, when I do it I need their internal consent. As fragile as the physical world is, the mind is a powerful piece of technology. The mind will usually do everything in its power to fight me, put up every wall it can to block me out like a virus; that is, unless they let their guard down. The easiest way to move around this is to work with people who are unconscious or in very small, slow increments.

It's possible to take somebody's soul with all walls up but it takes an immense amount of concentration and power, I don't even know if I have the ability to affect somebody's soul without their mental agreement. Instead, I'll stick to what I'm doing now.

As the train rolls its way towards the edge of the barren road I walk up and down the aisles. Nobody suspects what I'm doing, nobody can feel it but me. As I pass every passenger, slowly, I trade the smallest increment of their soul that I can muster. Such a small amount that their minds don't even trigger a response, a small enough portion that they won't even know I did it. They shouldn't be affected in any significant way, but it piles up for me. The small amount of soul I take from every healthy passenger is building a fortress in my chest, I can feel my powers coming back to me.

But souls have side effects.

I can feel myself changing. Everything about me is slowly beginning to change, I'm mentally morphing into a new person made up of dozens of new people.

A person's soul is what makes them the person they are. Our bodies, our minds, they're not what controls our emotion; rather, they simply act as a transmitter for our souls to carry into the physical world. A soul is useless in the real world by itself, it must bind itself to something powerful that is stationed within reality. A soul doesn't have the physical shape or characteristics to exist within human perception but our brains make wonderful houses for our souls. Human minds offer plenty of options, plenty of ways to act, different ways to think, different strengths, weaknesses, it's like a soul's playhouse; they're in their best habitat when they have more ways to express themselves. Souls, in a way, have something sort of like a coding, like a set of keys that are exclusive to that soul, an infinite string of numbers. When a soul enters the real world within a physical body, the body interprets as much as it can based on its real world limitations and translates it into a person. Some people are genuinely amazing or terrible people at heart, it's based on the way the characteristics of their inner essence. All the brain really does is interpret that and translate it.

While holding onto so many other souls I can feel my body begin to change. My emotion, the way I feel, every single mannerism I make. I suddenly become more nervous, more confident, angry, happy; just utterly conflicted. My feelings begin to skyrocket and plummet over and over again.

Focusing on my emotions has set my body into autopilot, I walk up and down the aisles taking a little bit of everyone and giving a little bit to everyone. I feel so odd giving out bits and pieces of broken soul and taking healthy slices from others but somebody is counting on me. We have a plan to execute, I need to do this. I need my power for this one.

When I finally sit back down Jayden looks at me. Nodding to me, I take the last bit of soul I'll need before I'm back to normal, *better* than normal. I'm sustaining no more than a single soul's worth in my body right now. Although, if I consume a quantity with higher worth than a single essence, it'll create more power that I'll be able to control. It's addicting, I don't want to stop, I can feel raw power coursing through my blood, through my nerves. I can feel myself getting stronger. It makes me want more.

This isn't something I can get addicted to, I can't keep going with this, *I can't let my emotions get the best of me.* I look back up to Jayden but he looks away again pretending like he doesn't know me. Collecting myself, I begin to take a little bit of soul from Jayden. For this plan, he won't need all of it, he's loaning me power right now.

I can feel myself hit a wall so intensely that my mind starts to ache. The barrier is solid, this barrier is Jayden's will, his inner psyche. I have no need, nor ability, to knock his guards down; after a couple seconds I can feel the gates open. He's granting me his consent. I look at him, "Are you sure about this, Jayden?"

Jayden doesn't say a word but rather nods to me, his glare is icy and strong as he stares out the window. I take a deep breath and begin to drain his soul.

Stay focused.

There's a very specific amount to take here, I can't stop early, I can't take too much. A person's soul quantity affects them immensely; although more soul generally grants an influx of mental power, it can become extremely harmful after while. The same goes for not having enough, but rather withers a person over time.

I count to five. One... Two... Three...

I want to keep going. It feels like I should take *all* of it, like my natural instincts are pushing me towards going through with the whole thing. Four... *No.* It takes all of me to slow down, I'm almost done. But do I have to stop so soon? There's so much power, there's so much to take and it's so beautiful.

It's as if I'm walking through an open field; the longer I walk the prettier the scenery gets. The distance between me and the dark, stormy skies behind me subtly grows. The wafting smell of vanilla and honey becomes stronger as I proceed, the voices in my head begin to quiet down. Instead, it's me in my head; nobody else. No pulling, no torment, no more pain. Finally, I feel freedom ahead.

Five. I come to an instant halt, pulling myself out of Jayden's body. That's all I needed, that's all I want. Stop here, this part of the plan is done. I look over to him, "Are you feeling okay?"

He nods, his eyes begin to squint a little, "Little light headed, but I'll be fine."

His soul changes me. I feel courageous, I feel stronger, I feel protective. I feel scared. Scared for those I love, I feel worried about the kids, the ones I was protecting two days ago. An utter sense of guilt begins to flood me; the faces of despair that I turned my back on begin to haunt me. Watching me, I can hear Rose's sobs in my head again. Logan's body limp on the floor, Victoria's arms wrapped around me. It all hurts, my chest tightens and it feels like I'm choking.

I try to mold my soul back to its original form, back to how mine was a couple days ago. Using all of my mental energy, I craft my soul back into mine, *Mason's*. Souls may be made of keys but I'm the locksmith. As a Striker, I have my soul's coding burned into my memory for the rest of eternity, it's not something I can forget. Back to normal, my soul is just like what it used to be but bigger. Much bigger. Much stronger, but still *Mason's*.

Yet, the remorse doesn't go away.

"This is a big deal, Mason," Jayden says without moving his glare from the glass, "I hope you're prepared." I look down and around myself, I'm not sure if I am. Am I prepared to do this right now? I'm terrified, nervous, shaking even but I lie to Jayden, "I'm ready. No sweat."

He gives me a subtle smile, I hope I can give him a bit of reassurance. I'm not getting any, I know that for sure.

After what feels like years, the train begins to slow down. Oh, God, this is it. This is where we get off, I can see big red letters scroll on and off the sides of the screen above us, "Rogue Street Station." The brakes squeal in anger as they try to stop the weight of the train; the train that's heading straight towards the beginning, this is how we're going to save them. We're leading an onslaught with an army of two.

I don't know why it hits me now, but I feel really connected to you guys. It feels like I've known you all for so long but never seen you, never heard your voice. It feels like I know everything about you, like I could answer any question about you with pinpoint accuracy, but the truth is, I really know nothing. I wish I could know more... I can't wait to know more.

My empathy rises, it's almost like they stole my thoughts. The voice, *my* voice in my head, echoes. Perhaps they're saying exactly what I was thinking.

I couldn't agree more! I'll be there soon.

I mentally stutter for a second. Why did they reply to themselves? That's odd, they took it like they weren't the ones saying it. The ethereal that's been trying to find us for so long said it, I'm certain of it. They replied like somebody else said it.

Did *I* say it?

Oh my God, I think I said that. It sounded like exactly what I was thinking because it *was* exactly what I was thinking. The first statement in my head was me, I was using my own voice just like all the other ethereals do. I need to do it again, I need to figure out how to communicate. They didn't know it was me, they probably thought it was Theodore, the one they've been talking to for the past few weeks. Maybe because we're in such similar directions, I need to tell them there's more than one of us. I need to tell them they're in danger.

"Jayden! I just-" I'm cut off, Jayden gets up, the train has stopped. He looks at me, "We have to go." I hesitate, he's right. I won't need to communicate if I just stick to the plan, we can do this. We'll be here to protect them, I don't need to warn them because they're not walking into danger. They're walking towards safety, I'm always going to be there to protect them.

I don't think I finished fixing my soul, I'm thinking of things Jayden would probably say.

There's something I'm missing. As Jayden and I walk off the train I ponder to myself, what am I doing wrong? Why can't I speak to them? They're using my voice, why can't *I* use my voice?

Although it stopped us on Rogue Street, the alleyway where we plan to meet is a mile North on the closed road. Even though it's shut down, though, there doesn't seem to be heavy guarding around the barriers; only a couple guards are patrolling. Slipping through the outskirts should be the easiest option; we could use Jayden's jumping ability but that would leave too big of a signal.

So we climb.

We slip into the crowd and start roaming towards an area where we're alone. Waiting for an opportune moment, we jump up a steel ladder leading up to the back staircase of an abandoned apartment complex. Climbing up the railings and hiding in as much shadow as we can find in the sunlight, we make our way to the top of the ten story building.

Staying low on top of the roof, we tip-toe towards the edge where we can scope out the city. Several blocks are completely empty, more than just Rogue Street. There's nobody for as far as I can see; there's guarded blockades at the end of each road and each soldier is armed. Every building is empty, many have become rundown and unkempt. Doesn't seem like anybody sees us.

Walking up the sidewalk, Jayden stays totally silent. I can't tell if he's worried or concentrating, perhaps both. He's in more danger than I am, he's missing a chunk of his soul, a chunk of his power. He's never been in that situation before, he doesn't know what that's like; he has no practice fighting with only part of him as far as I know. I'm sure he'll learn quickly, but I don't know if there will be any time to learn.

Jayden suddenly stops, "Okay, Mason," he says, his neck tense but his head planted on a swivel, "I'm going to get to the alley, I'll zap my way there. You stay here until it's time, okay?"

I nod in agreement, I look at him, then back forward. I pat him on the back a couple times. I want to console him but I'm not very confident myself. As my hand falls, Jayden disappears. Within the blink of an eye he's gone, nothing but a small cloud of smoke where he used to stand. I couldn't hear a thing except a small spark of electricity. Off in the distance I can see small flashes of light; if I didn't know any better I would imagine it came from a street light or malfunctioning sign, it's so subtle.

I leap down from the building, skipping down from rooftop to lower rooftop until I finally reach the concrete below. The tension in my ankles grows tight but I can easily endure. They'll be on his scent soon. I begin to run, sprint, it feels like flying. I've never been able to run this fast before, it feels good. I can feel the cool wind ruffling through my hair; if a car drove by me I'd beat it there. I'm closing in on the sight, this would be my time to make a scene. For the quickest second, I believe deep in my heart that this might actually work, maybe we can solve the problems I've lived with my whole life. Maybe we can end this company once and for all.

My broken phone rings.

Stopping in my tracks, skidding along the pavement, I pull my phone out of my pocket. My hands begin to shake, my heart pounds heavy in my chest. If there was anything that would destroy this plan, it would come from a phone call; I'm sure of it.

It's Rose.

Without even taking a second thought I drag my hand across the screen, I can instantly hear heavy breathing. She yells into the phone before I can even put it to my ear, "*Mason!*"

I choke on my words; I don't know what to say. A fluttering sense of guilt and tension builds in my throat, blocking my words.

She pants before she can choke up another word, "Mason, we need you. They're here, *they're here*! *They're at the facility*!" She sounds skittish and she sounds terrified. What can I do? Jayden needs me right now, if I run away, Jayden will be all alone with an entire company out and ready to capture him and he only has part of his soul right now. He's out there jumping from location to location just waiting to be attacked. He doesn't even have all of his power, he's counting on me. He's counting on me so much that he gave me part of his spiritual existence. If I run away now, I'll be running away with a piece of Jayden.

"Rose, can you-" I'm interrupted, the phone just hung up. They're in danger and they're crying for my help. What do I do, Mason, think... *Think!*

CHAPTER IX

ROSE'S RESCUE

Robert did so much for me as a kid; hell, he's done so much for me even today. I wouldn't be who I am now if it wasn't for him, I don't even know if I'd be alive.

It wouldn't be hard to say that the saddest moment of my life was losing him; the only thing that could hold a torch would be the death of my childhood friend. I cried for days, weeks even, I never got over it. If I had the tears for it I'd still be crying over him. The man didn't deserve what he got, he deserved the world. Why the hell can't people just understand that? Why can't people take a second to think before they do things?

And on my birthday, even.

On my 16th birthday, Robert took me down to show me a surprise he had prepared for me; I never figured out what it was. When we got around the corner, three men stood in place of the gift which then stood in pieces of cardboard, paper, and tattered pieces of arts and crafts. Together they stomped and demolished it; as we walked by we grabbed their attention. The moment we stepped foot, the moment I made eye contact with those heartless bastards, Robert spoke to me, only me; he told me, "*Run.*"

I don't know what's worse, hearing the words or not listening. I guess in my head I saw myself protecting him, protecting *us*.

Fury filled my eyes. The anger consumed me and I snapped. I grabbed the closest junkie by the collar of his leather jacket, his sharp gaze was intensified by the tattoos under his eyes. His confident look dissipated completely when I smashed his skull in with my head; a loud *crack* and blood began to pour from a hole in his buzz cut. His eyes rolled into his head as he began to seize up, his two lackeys utterly terrified.

Everything was in slow motion for me. I could feel my heart beating faster and faster but the men in front of me were only getting slower. This was nothing close to what it's like in the ring. There's no respect, there's no honor here. There's nothing but anger and pain.

Like I was walking on coals, the heat and temper in my body only rose. The other two pulled small handguns out of their baggy pants but I didn't even waver. I grabbed the barrel of the left man's gun and ripped it right out of his hands as if a child was holding it. With a single swift motion, I lifted the firearm and brought it down on the crook of the man's neck. I could hear, feel something breaking in his body; the sound was so satisfying at the time. Choking and spitting blood, he fell to the ground heaving for air. I gave a murderous glare to the man on my right and his knees nearly buckled. He didn't have the balls to shoot me, neither of them did.

Time begins to roll by me like the wind, slow and cold. I take a single step towards the man, I can smell the soil of his sweatpants, I can see the terror in his eyes.

I hear clunking from the ground behind me.

Red wanted to run but he was waiting for me. He skipped out of his safety to watch me transform into the demonic personification of myself. The moment I gazed back the only thing I could hear was two gunshots firing off, two deafening booms behind me. I stopped dead in my tracks, I see Red slowly topple over like a tree, freshly cut. Blood began to spill from his shoulder and neck, he didn't even have time to say another word. He didn't even get a chance to speak. In my head I screamed, in my head I wailed and cried and threw the biggest tantrum in the world. In my head, I was a little kid, dying on the inside.

But all I could do was watch.

The two men who survived picked up their weapons and ran away, blood trailed from the throat of the one I pistol whipped. The man with a hole in his head, lifeless and limp... But I wasn't conscious enough to care about any of them.

I sat there in shambles, denying the truth of what had just happened. It felt like the blood that poured from his body was the shimmers of my imagination, like the tattered pieces of construction paper and cardboard were the tattered pieces of a nightmare I was having.

But it was all too real.

I ran away from my problems, I ran away from the goddamn psychopaths that killed my only friend, the only family I had in this world. I ran away from the psychopath that I had become. It wasn't fair; it's not fair. There was one thing in this world that made me happy, there was one thing I remember keeping me going in that time, and without getting a chance to speak, he was gunned down in his own city.

He didn't have a home, but Red and I both knew that we were home together, roof or no roof.

Pissed, enraged, livid with anger, I ran down to the fight clubs, I let my sheer rage out through my fists. I was relentless, I'm afraid I may have permanently hurt somebody down there; the truth is that I felt like I needed to. I wasn't ready to keep living life, but if I was going to, I was hurting *something*. Opponent after opponent, blood, sweat, and loose teeth began to pile up on the fighting grounds. It was the most money I ever made on that floor, but this time, I didn't want it. I didn't even care for it, I wanted Red back. Nothing can get Red back, nothing will ever give me my family back. I can't forgive those who killed my only friend, I can't forgive myself for being the reason he died, and I'll never stop resenting the day Robert and I went home for my birthday.

That was when he found me, three years into my despair. Sticking out like a sore thumb, a man in a nicely-tailored suit dressed in all black; from his shoes to his undershirt, an elaborate stitching of dark fabric. Fight after fight, I let my anger get the best of me for hours on end and he watched the whole thing. When I decided I was done, when I decided that fighting didn't help and nothing was going to, I walked off the fighting floor and he approached me.

"I need your help," he said. Pulling a card from his jacket, "I work for a secret organization of specialized agents. I believe that your skill sets would be a major help." He extended his arm out to hand me is stupid, dreaded card, *Dragon Tech Incorporated*.

I begin to run in the opposite direction, I run as fast as I can. I can only run this fast because Jayden *gave* me a piece of himself and now my back is turned towards him. He's vulnerable and putting himself in a position where he is a target, where he's out in the open, where he can make a scene big enough that he's sure they'll see it.

I try to convince myself that this is what he'd want.

The original plan stated that I would meet him nearby, cause the biggest scene I could with loud bangs, ripping buildings apart, blowing up signs, whatever it took to gather as many people from outside as possible. Jayden would make a scene unto himself, crying out, screaming that he had a heart attack on the outskirts of the barren district. He would even electrocute himself to create an audience. Nobody knows about the empowered world of ethereals or surreals yet, and the first person who would hate that information out first would be Theodore. His illegal business runs on privacy, staying underground, below everybody's radar. If he comes by while dozens of people gather around, the only thing he can do is watch within the crowd.

Then I could walk up behind him and kill him where he stands.

I would do it via bargaining. In order to keep myself alive during the process, I would've had to slowly drain myself of my own soul by putting small increments into the dozens of people around, not enough to change them immensely but more than enough to give me room for *all* of his soul, enough to end the man's life.

I'm so excited guys, I'm a mile away! So close!

No, this can't be happening.

As I'm running towards the facility, I'm halfway there already, the voices in my head inform me that I may have already passed them; I may not have only killed one friend, I may have killed the one I was trying to save as well. I pull out my phone, my fingers working as fast as I can get them to. I can't stop messing up, the sweat on my fingers is playing with my broken screen.

I try so hard to get a message across to Jayden, tell him to abort the mission, run, get away from there. To hide. Jayden, please, of all things, see my message. Please, just stay alive. I can't lose you, I'm not willing to lose anybody else.

Placing the phone back in my pocket I keep running. I run faster, faster than my limits would ever allow me. I can feel myself getting exhausted but I don't care; I ignore the pain in my lungs and run faster. Rose, Victoria, Logan; this will be my redemption. I *will* protect them.

I know if Jayden had to choose between himself and his brother, Logan would always come first.

Yet, I know that I'm really only doing this for myself, for the satisfaction of soothing out my past. Like one justice will undo my injustices.

I turn around the last corner, the most suburban area in the city; I see a large field and in the distance, the facility. I hesitate, stutter, then slow down. I'm not in hyperdrive anymore, I'm jogging. There are huge black vans parked out in front of the facility, men in suits are placed around the building, standing at the entrance, around the cars and a couple around the sides.

For the first time, the most hateful face I've ever seen gave me more relief than I've ever felt before; standing before the doors are two men, Theodore and his right hand man.

Why are they here? They're not coming for Jayden, maybe he's going to survive. I take a sigh of relief, but I'm not done yet. There's a reason they're here and that means all the kids here are in danger. I don't know why they suspected this place, why they choose to be here over sniffing out Jayden who just escaped… This can't be good.

Getting closer I can see the main staff standing outside the doors talking to the boss. I approach them both, "Hey, what's going on here?" The ethereal pull I feel from him grows so strong that it feels like I could grab the invisible rope pulling me in. It makes my stomach turn and grind into knots.

He looks at me, raising one eyebrow, I must've interrupted him, "Mason, what're you doing here?"

His voice gives me chills, "I was scouting an area about a couple miles from here. I heard there was some," I pause for a second as if I'm worried about the staff learning what I'm speaking of, "business to be had." I lie to him, I need to be really quick on my wits, now.

"Hm," he looks at me. It seems like he's taking his time on whether or not he should believe me. Quickly, he looks back at the staffer, "We have reason to believe that there's a Code 0-0-1 here; although it seems to appear and swiftly disappear on occasion… Odd for something so strong."

I look at him, a Code 001 is the most powerful form of anomaly on record. Thinking to myself I pretend like I'm thinking aloud, "I can go scout it out if you want."

He stops, looking at me. If I didn't know any better, I would think he just smiled. "Sure, let's go scout it out."

My heart drops into my stomach, that's not the response I was expecting. Theodore spins around and looks behind him, "Mr. Parker, you stay here and keep watch." His right hand man looks at him sternly giving him a quick nod of approval. I look at the staffer, give her a quick nod, then walk inside. Her face is stern but her eyes are screaming at me. I try my best to speak through my expression, "Don't worry, you'll be fine."

Mr. Parker? Parker is my last name.

I walk in first, as far ahead of him as I can. Through the double doors and down the stairs, we reach a basement area, the secondary cafeteria, where many of the kids normally stay during the middle of the day. I turn the corner before my boss can reach me and wrap my hand around the wall; feeling around, I pick up the scan breaker I placed when I was here. Shoving it in my pocket, I stand like I'm waiting for the director to approach, hands in my pockets. Looking around, the kids and lower staff begin to recognize me with confused expressions. Where are they?

The director walks down the steps at about the same time Rose, Victoria, and Logan walk downstairs from the gym. I'm satisfied to see they're okay but I'm sure they're very distraught. I can already see Victoria's face turning to anger, I have a feeling Rose is calming her down right now. I look at my boss then back at the kids and speak in a booming voice, "Sorry to bother all of you, but I was wondering if any of you have seen any... Strange activity?"

I would shake my head but that would be too obvious. Instead, I give one person a message, the one person who I know can read it, *Don't let anybody use their powers. As far as anybody is concerned, this is a normal orphanage.*

She doesn't say anything back but the tension in her face tells me that she understands what I'm planning. Rose read my mind, she knows what I'm saying, she's telling everybody else as fast as she can. Even the staffer can hear her, she looks back at Rose, hides it by looking around the room as if she was looking at everybody the first time, finally looking back us while she shakes her head, "N-no..." Everybody turns to look at her as she breaks the silence, I can see the courage she's building up slowly turn to fruition. Slowly growing on the crowd, everybody begins to shake their heads in agreement. Light mumbles fill the room, "No, I haven't seen anything," and "Nuh uh."

The director takes a step in front of me, "Then I'm sure you wouldn't mind us looking around? Perhaps asking a few questions?"

The room falls totally silent. The staffer shakes her head, "Go ahead." She looks very professional but I can tell she's scared. In the corner of my eyes I can see Rose shaking relentlessly. If anything happens, if somebody dropped a binder, a book, if somebody hit the table too hard, she'd turn invisible. She can't give us away, I shoot her a look, "Rose, you have to go to the bathroom. Ask if you can go to the bathroom."

She doesn't even ask, she stands up from the table and walks halfway to the front desk, "Mrs. Markus?" The staff member at the catering booth looks over to her, the director making his way around the room, "May I go to the bathroom?"

Mrs. Markus looks utterly confused, dumbfounded at such an outspoken request from such a quiet girl, but with hesitation agrees. Rose speed walks over to the stairs. I grab the director's attention, "Hey, sir?" Quickly, he moves his attention over to me. I hear his foot stomp the ground profusely. It echoes through the room, on the way up the stairs I watch Rose vanish.

I see his glare snap away from where Rose is but his eyes are in her direction, "Would you like me to check anywhere?"

The director looks around as he silently pauses, "Actually… That would be perfect. You look, I'll ask questions." He makes his way, going through openings in the kids and around tables, to Mrs. Markus. Her face is pudgy and her figure is stout. I can see sweat making the surface of his forehead shiny, her curly red hair is beginning to get frizzy. His icy glare stares bullets through her but she keeps some composure. Pretending to investigate the area, I listen in on their conversation. I don't have anybody to read my mind right now, I can't help her.

Logan is my next biggest problem. When his emotions get the best of him sometimes sparks will ignite on his body. Electricity will even arc between his fingertips. I shoot him a glare, but he'll never know what I'm trying to say like this.

Don't worry, I'll tell him, I hear inside my head. I look up the inner entrance, Rose is camping on the stairs right now, she never actually left. I look over as Logan lowers his hands below his legs out of sight. God, she's a genius.

Logan's body has grown even more frail than before, the bruises on his body have spread and his eyes are bloodshot. He looks like a flu patient who was just pulled from bed… But he seems okay.

When I turn back to look, I see that I missed the whole conversation. Theodore looks like he's trying to wrap things up, his voice is less intimidating than before, as if he got the answers he wanted.

"Where were you?" she asks me through my own mind. I don't move my glare, but I attempt to respond.

"Rogue Street, and that's hopefully where I'm going right after this." I look around, trying not to look at the stairs, "Stay away from me."

She falls silent, I'm sure she got the message.

The director gestures me towards him, "Mason, I think we're done here." He begins up the stairs. As he goes up, I hide my arm behind the wall as I place the scan breaker back again; I attach it to the wall almost silently. I can hear it subtly deploying.

"Actually, wait a minute," he suddenly says, spinning around. My hands stop as fast as they can, but the scan breaker is already setting up shop right now. It'll take about a minute to deploy. If I pull it off the wall, it'll bust the machine and make a *lot* of noise. The director looks right at me, "Mason, can you do me a favor?"

"Sure thing, sir," I do my best to keep my composure and a hardened glare as he talks to me. "Whatever you need.

"Can you get some contact info from this place before you go?" I nod in agreement; he smirks at me before he makes his way back up the stairs. I can tell he knows more than I want him to. Before retreating with him I grab a slip of paper and write down their phone number and email.

Don't worry, Mason. Jayden and I are okay, come meet us on Rogue Street!

CHAPTER X

OUR CHANCE TO FIGHT

What the hell are they doing!? That message is going straight to both of us, does she not know she's in danger yet? Theodore doesn't react.

When we open the glass doors, most of the people have left. All that stayed with us is one black van and its driver who stands outside, composed and well dressed, right in front of it. He has sunglasses on; an earpiece curling out behind his ear, tucking away into his collar. My director walks towards the vehicle but he abruptly stops, "Mason, I'd like you to come with us."

I halt. Suddenly, I'm terrified, "Why is that, sir?"

Ignoring me, he resumes his walk over to the car, the driver now taking his place in the driver's seat. I hesitantly take my seat just behind my director, closing my door; my thoughts are racing right now, I'm terrified.

I give myself a second before I let the relief and anxiety rush through my body. Jayden is okay, the ethereal is right next to him, and they've met safely but now Theodore is aware of a good chunk of our plan. I couldn't even begin to take a big enough sigh in order to explain my emotions. It feels like, even though our plan fell through, everything is falling into place.

I instantly second guess myself as we turn onto Rogue Street.

The black van approaches the guarded barricades. With the pull of a lever, the barricades slowly move out of the way, allowing the vehicle's passage. We're going towards the alley Jayden was hiding. I try to stay quiet but the questions burst out of me, "Where are we going, sir?"

He looks at me through the mirror, "Don't worry, Mason. I just wanted an extra hand."

I think I just peed a little.

Up the street, several black vehicles just like ours are surrounding the alleyway. Three men in dark suits are surrounding Jayden and another, their hands in the air. I can't make the details of the second person out, that must be the ethereal.

I can't believe it. They found them. While we were in the facility, they went out looking for them. Damn it, I really did fail Jayden, didn't I? What the hell am I going to do? What the hell *can* I do?

How could I let this happen?

As we stop, parking on the sidewalk across from the action, the director and I walk out of our vehicle. Following the same motion, Mr. Parker leaves his car a few yards down the street, waiting for the director to show up by his side. We cross the street, meeting up with him, finally taking our place in the thick of things. I look at Jayden helplessly, I don't know what to do, what can I do? I can't even think, I can feel my insides shriveling up, I feel totally useless. Looking around, there's five men against us three, they're equipped and we're unarmed. We have power, yes, but I don't even know what one of our powers are.

I look over at her, the ethereal that's been in my head for so long now. She came here looking for somebody, looking for a friend she lost long ago; perhaps one she never met. She comes here getting drawn and quartered, she's probably confused and terrified. I can see her looking around.

Actually, it looks more like she's scoping the place out.

What's going on right now? Who are these people? I'm surrounded right now, I have my hands up in surrender, I don't know what they want, they won't talk.

I'm dying inside. I want to cry, scream, flail, I can't do anything but watch. Jayden is giving me a glare of, I can only guess, hatred and resentment. The guy who has only given to me now watches as I sit, motionless. I can't help it, what can I do?

"Subdue them," I hear his sinister words hit my ears; I shutter. Slowly, the men begin to close in simultaneously. I can't control myself, I have to. Suddenly, without a briefing, without a moment of warning, my anger reaches its maximum and breaches the surface. My sorrow, my wallowing, it's gone; it's been turned into blind rage, I'm absolutely livid.

"*NO!*" I cry out with fury, I rush out elbowing one of the men in the back of the neck. Falling to the ground, I quickly change my footing and dash left; I drop my shoulder. Sliding inches underneath his chin, I lift my body up as fast as I can into him, my shoulder catching his chest guard and lifting him feet into the air before gravity has its way with him. As he hits the ground I listen to his struggle for air mixed with the cracking of his bones.

I'm stabbed, my skin is penetrated, I feel two shards enter my back. It's a feeling I've felt before; it's electricity. A mad current runs through my body, the pain only makes me angrier. I'm not letting this put me down, I've been through this way too many times to even be phased.

In one swift movement I swipe away the chords that are biting into my skin. I wrap the twine around my hand and yank the weapon out of Mr. Parker's hands. Letting go of the trigger, the current ends.

Wham!

I feel something hit me in the back of the head, a throbbing sensation rushes through me. The third man has butted me with the end of his taser, my head stings but I don't have time to feel pain right now. A flash out of the corner of my eye reveals that Jayden and the ethereal are gone. Relief washes over me.

Suddenly my punches soften. My anger lowers, my face pales. I can see the two men getting back up, somebody swipes at my feet. I fall over, toppling onto my back. I feel a kick make its way to my ribs. Pain is trampling over me, another two shards infiltrate my skin, four shards. The electric current is getting less and less bearable, I'm really struggling to move, now. I try to make my arms move around to the chords but I get another kick to the hip; I yelp in pain.

I can't do anything, I can't help myself. I did what I wanted to do, I got Jayden and the girl out of here safe. As long as they're safe, I'm happy. The kids are safe, I'll sit here and take whatever beating they can dish out.

I probably deserve this, anyways.

I slowly close my eyes in satisfaction as pain eats me alive. I can deal with this, I'm happy with this. I've lived my whole life in pain, pain is a good friend of mine at this point. Pain doesn't hurt me anymore, I find comfort in it. There's no reason to get up.

Wallowing in my sorrow, I hear loud battering noises. Noises like punching, kicking, but I don't feel anything. Am I totally numb now? Have they kicked the ends of my nerves off? Slowly, I open my eyes. The tasers have stopped and I see them, now, lying on the ground as the men frantically look around. I see one of them swing through the air helplessly but a figure quickly appears behind, knocking him into the ground.

Is Jayden doing this? Whoever is doing this is disappearing and reappearing but I don't see any sparks, no flashes of light. Just subtle appearances of a single person. Again, the figure appears and it definitely isn't Jayden.

I can feel myself tugged towards him, when he disappears, the tugging goes away. Appearing again, he deals another blow to one of the armed guards, straight to the jaw. The invisible rope grows tighter.

It's a half-ethereal.

CHAPTER XI

LIGHTS IN PLANE SIGHT

Before today, I'd never even seen another ethereal in my life. Now there's three standing around me. My tugging grows stronger, the ropes that pull me towards every ethereal is suddenly pulling my limbs apart. My director, the one who is currently fleeing with Mr. Parker, hops into another vehicle. Before I can even get up, the vehicle skids off, I can feel the rope that pulls me in towards him like it's attached to the car he's in.

Switching my attention over to the battle at hand I see two men are knocked out and one is stumbling around in a daze. One more mystical reappearance and a good knock to the temple sends him to the concrete. Looking up, he doesn't disappear this time. He looks at me, offering me his hand through his heavy breathing. So many questions to ask, so much I need to know, but nothing to say. I look at him, lower my voice to a whisper; I take his hand, "You're an ethereal, too?"

He helps me up. He's older than me, perhaps late twenties. He looks me dead in the eyes, the light reflecting off of his pupils, they're bright green; bright but lethal, "You're the one who's been talkin' in my head this whole time?"

I shake my head. His accent is subtle but noticeably southern. Dark brown hair sprouts from his chin, a small beard and moustache, pretty well kept. His hair is messy and curled but controlled. His body is very muscular, I can see his biceps pressed against the fabric sleeves of his rolled up flannel. "N-no, that was somebody else. I came here looking for her, she was just," I take a second to cough, "here." I look down trying to catch my breath, "My friend helped her escape, she was the one in the center of the guys before I was."

"You know where they are now?" His face is cold and stern, his jaw sharp. His words are frigid but nothing like Theodore's. He's respectable, he speaks with passion, not hate.

"No idea," I say shaking my head. He's taller than me, quite a bit. I look up to meet his gaze, "What are you? I mean I know what you are but what *are* you?"

He pats me on the back as he turns around and walks away from me, "We dun' got time for standin', let's walk and talk, bud."

Walking up Rogue Street, he explains it all to me. His name is Gavin; he's a Walker, somebody who can shift between realities within the blink of an eye. I've never truly understood the idea, and to be honest, I don't really now, either. According to him, "There's an infinite number o' planes on Earth, each parallel to each other," whatever that means. Kind of like thousands of giant spheres, three dimensional objects that coexist within each other. Each sphere is another dimension, another universe right atop ours. He references to our reality, the one we currently stand on, as the martial realm. The most life inhabits it, it's the middle ground of all the realities. Other realities exist in extremities, it's the reason we can't see them.

"We can't see, sniff, or fondle anything that ain't on our dimension. If something's from another reality, it dun' exist to us. If somethin' switches planes it'll seem like it's just gone." When he disappears and reappears randomly, he's walking from plane to plane.

"Could you hear the voices, too?" I ask after a brief silence.

"To be totally honest with ya', they keep me awake," he explains to me. "But ever since I heard that voice, I took the first aircraft here. The family lives back in Arkansas but I live alone. My wife left me a while ago, I only see my kids durin' the holidays, I dun' have much to lose. I didn't never pay enough attention to scc that there were more of us. When I found out, I had to come."

I can't help but sympathise. The feeling is so hard to resist, impossible to ignore. Nobody would be able to stay silent if they went so long with a rope around their waist and voices in their head asking them to get closer.

Suddenly, a flash of light hits the corner of my eye deep in an alley behind me. I know exactly who that must be. I run in to see but I stop dead in my tracks. Following behind the half-ethereal stops seconds later, raising one eyebrow, "Problem, bud?"

I hold a finger up, "Hold on." I listen, looking around. I switch my abilities around, my senses grow keen. I listen in to everything, a mile away I can hear a horn honking in rage, I can hear a mouse skitter across the sidewalk. Where is he? I'm looking for another flash of light.

Nothing. I don't hear a thing. Maybe he's standing in the alley, maybe he's hiding out. I motion the half-ethereal to come with me. He follows without question.

I don't know what it is but this odd bond we share is one I've never felt before. It doesn't necessarily induce trust but I feel it much easier to trust him. By the way he follows me, I think the feeling is mutual.

Peering around the corner I don't really see anything. A large green dumpster is the only thing peeking out, at the end of the alley is a wall, another building from another street. Where the hell could he have gone?

I smell something. It's difficult because there's somebody next to me and the dumpster's pungent odor but I narrow it down as well as I can. There's somebody else here, I smell burning. More than one person, that's gotta be him.

I hear a loud bang against the dumpster. It has to be him, I know it is. Running around to the side, I finally catch a glimpse.

It's Logan.

CHAPTER XII

A BROTHERHOOD
OF NO REALITY

Piled together, hiding behind a giant dumpster in the alley, are four kids. Victoria, Logan, Rose, and another; a girl that looks exactly like Victoria, *exactly* like Victoria, but with opposite colored clothing and vibrant purple eyes. Unlike Victoria's black dressings, dark skirt with thick framed glasses and black lace gloves, Victoria-2 is wearing a white skirt that is somehow magically not dirty, white lace gloves, and bright pink glasses. As they sit next to each other I smell the disdain they radiate for each other. Ah, friendship.

Those eyes… Where have I seen them before?

My emotions pile on top of each other they almost mold together. I feel more numb than excited, "How did you guys get here?"

They all simultaneously shrug; Logan has no idea what ability he used, I'm sure he has no idea how to use it again. I want to find Jayden, maybe I can shoot him a text. I pull up my phone, the cracked screen is still radiating a bright shade of purple, brighter than before. *Jayden, I'm in an alley farther North on Rogue, in between the hardware shop and the Thai place, meet me here. There's something I want to show you.*

The information I leave out is a test, does he still trust me? I want to know if he thinks I've let him down. While I wait, I introduce my new friend to the kids, "Gavin, these are the hoodlums, hoodlums, meet Gavin."

Gavin looks quizzically at me and the group of kids. It's not hard to miss that I skipped over one of them with my gestures; honestly, I have no idea who she is. He points to her, "Who's the Metamorph?" Suddenly, her eyes widen and everybody, including me, looks at her. I think Gavin just ratted somebody out. Thoughts come to my mind, the biggest one being: *what have these kids been doing?*

I knew she was familiar, she's a shapeshifter. She's my goddamn taxi driver. And my *cat* for that matter.

I try to organize my thoughts and my emotions but they've seem to have vacated me completely. I feel hollow.

A see a gleam in my peripheral. Jayden and the ethereal girl stand behind me, Jayden glaring down at me. I shudder a little bit, purposely blocking Logan from his vision, "I want to show you-"

"Not here," he interrupts. I suddenly grab Gavin and Logan by the arm, both look at me with a confused gaze but I don't waiver. Jayden quickly puts a hand on my shoulder; off we go. Static ignites in my ear, my vision goes white for a split second. We're underground. I can't tell where underground, it looks sort of like a sewer but with no water. Everybody in the group except the four who understand jumping, me, Jayden, my human cat, and the ethereal girl, begin to question what just happened, ask each other, and slowly turn into piles of jelly. I push myself to the side, allowing view between Logan and Jayden. Their expressions are simultaneous and exactly the same, instant overwhelming happiness floods them. They suddenly dash towards each other, Logan's motions a little off put by his inability to move effectively, wrapping arms around each other they yell in unison, "Where have you *been*!?"

"It's been months, I haven't heard from you!" Jayden cries out.

Together they share quick sentences, I see a gleam on Jayden's face. It's a tear creeping down his cheek. No need to mention it but I'm more than happy to see him like this. Logan as well, no exception. Their words come in quick succession, I can't tell how they can make out each other's sentences but they seem to be having a functional conversation of some sort.

As they chat I turn around to look at the shapeshifter. I ask the same question as Gavin, "Who's the Metamorph?" Victoria and Rose look at each other dumbfounded then back at the girl who is now cuddled up to herself attempting to hide from everybody with no hiding spot in sight. Rose finally looks at me with a reply, "This is Veronica, she's Victoria's twin."

I'm disappointed.

I furrow my brows and rub the space between my eyes in anguish, "Twin, huh? Named Veronica?" I look over at Victoria with a condescending pause, "I didn't think you could get any dumber," I snap my eyes to Rose without moving my head, "but I'd expect more from you."

Veronica gives me half-assed suspicious glare to hide her mild giggles beneath her breath. I look back over to the Veronica. I don't say a word but my glare at her intensifies. Staring daggers at her, she finally gives in. In conceding, the girl takes a deep breath, her body beginning to transform. Her skin looks like it's melting off and reforming, her hair straightens out and sinks into her scalp just a little, she even loses a couple inches of height. She finalizes as a short brunette girl with pale skin and straight hair to her shoulders, still wearing the same clothes and glasses. Taking her glasses off, she looks at Victoria who seems to have a little bit of an eye twitch by this point.

Suddenly, as if she was a volcano at its breaking point, Victoria erupts, "*You have got to be kidding me!*" Victoria goes on and on about a whole bunch of different ranting subjects, talking mostly in gibberish as her angry words begin to blur together, her voice slurred with anger. Veronica looks at me for some solitude but all I do is shrug and mouth to her, "Sorry," shaking my head with complacency.

Looks like everybody has plenty of explaining to do and very little time to do so.

Catching everybody up on everybody else's lives and recent events, including the fact that I knew where Logan was the whole time, we all sit in a little circle huddled together, explaining what happened and giving out mild introductions. Turns out that the kids went on a little adventure while I was gone, lead by a mischief making Metamorph shaped like a Mischeviant.

Metamorphs are a species of surreals that have the ability to change their appearance based on either creativity or somebody they've seen. She must have quite a bit of skill, perfecting somebody's look so well and keeping the act on for so long is no easy feat, she must really know what she's doing. And on a creepier note, she must have been watching Victoria for quite a while.

Gavin was probably able to tell so easily simply because of her eye color and the odd twin detail. Shapeshifters often have a small quirk that they have to keep the same between forms, eye color is a common one. The purple eyes on a copy of Victoria, there's not really a better answer.

The ethereal girl's name is Anastasia, Anna for short. 17 years old, she's two years younger than me. Turns out she lived in California, a few hundred miles South of us, but ran away from her uncle a couple weeks ago; according to her he's a pretty terrible dude, usually drunk, abusive, lots of bad things. She decided to go out and figure out who else is out there, just as the rest of us did, but little did she know that she was only one of two who knew how to speak out. As far as she thought, speaking to ethereals across the world was something we could all do.

Her hair is long and straight, reaching just to her waist, light brown but it shimmers a little orange in broad daylight. Freckles cover her nose and some of her cheeks, her eyes are a rich brown color and her features are soft and warm. She's very skinny, only a couple inches shorter than me.

Jayden and Logan went on together about what they've been

through, Jayden explaining his reason for working at the company and the skills he acquired at home; the ability to jump, specifically. Logan explained his completely accidental jump to the alley, how he couldn't move, how scared he was, all the things I felt when I experienced it the first time but this time with no tour guide like Jayden. Jayden was pretty psyched to see that he was able to do it at least once, he's been trying to teach him for a while; Logan didn't recognize the fact that he ever tried to teach him that but they both put it aside.

Victoria officially hates everybody in this group now but me and Veronica both seem like we're on her shit list. She sits in the corner with her normal Victoria pose, arms crossed, huddled up into herself, her toes pointed towards each other, her face angry and jealous. Her eyes are locked on me like she's ready to pounce.

After Gavin explained what I knew about him as well as his abilities as a half-ethereal, Rose showed us something new that *she* learned how to do. After looking around for a second, she takes focus on a small pebble that was laying on the ground; closing her eyes and taking a deep breath, the pebble begins to rumble, barely lifting off the ground. After raising in the air ever so slightly, it slowly sinks back down to the ground. Rose takes a deep exhale as she exhausts herself, her power is just beginning but it's impressive she got this far by herself. Turns out the Metamorph taught her about that power, helped her learn how to use it as well. As weird as she is and as creepy as her interactions with us are, she seems to be pretty helpful. Honestly, I'm in awe of how far she's gotten. When I met her, she was afraid to even scratch the surface of her abilities, now she's taking on feats way beyond her level. Her potential is off the charts.

It's almost hard to stay mad at them.

Almost.

After all is said and all is done I realize that I'm just glad everybody is safe. We found the ethereal we were looking for and another as well. We reached the kids, Jayden, and the new cat friend they picked up. Before I get around to asking how to get out of an abandoned sewer and what to do after *that*, since we'll probably get surrounded by Dragon Tech in an instant, I want one last question answered.

The excitement I should be feeling is extremely diluted if even there at all. I don't think anybody knows the true intensity of the situation at hand. Sure, it's great that everybody's together but that really just means we have the chance to die in each other's arms.

I want so badly to be happy but I can't get myself there. When we walk out we'll be ambushed, quartered, beaten to death or shot. We can't all make it out, especially with the living-deadweight kids. If anybody knows the power this company possesses it's me, and it's more than a thousand of us. My confidence is slowly flooding out of me, a somber sensation begins to envelope my body.

I look over at Anna, the other ethereal girl. I ask her, "How are you able to speak to all of us? Why can't I do that?"

She giggles a little bit, her voice is very soft and soothing, "You're over complicating it. Here's how it was explained to me," she says. She gets off her butt and shifts over to her knees, pointing her toes outwards and her knees inwards, using her hands to aid her words, "As ethereals, we share a lot of things, kind of like how surreals share reality in common. We don't share reality in common as much as they do, but we have other bonds, possibly even stronger bonds. The voice we hear when somebody speaks to us, when somebody sends a message to all of us, is *our* voice." I tilt my head in confusion. She continues on, "One of our many bonds is a voice that we all share, a voice that we each have inside our head. We can't talk at the same time because we're sharing the same singular vocals. Long ago, it wasn't used often because there were so many more ethereals. I believe there were more voices to share back then, but I can't know that..." She begins to trail off for a second but she jumps back in. "Either way, I know that it's important to understand that you're not alone when you speak. When you communicate to us, use us in your message. Use our collective voice, not your own."

Her words of wisdom dumbfound me, all these things have been hiding under my belt and I had no idea they even existed. She's been speaking directly into my ear for who knows how long and I'm just now figuring out what this means. Us ethereals are a network, a connected species hiding behind a curtain of reality, the bonds we share is a hundred times stronger than blood, yet today was the first day that I've met a single one.

I focus myself, one collected mind, one collective voice. I think like I'm using the voice that she used to speak to me, her voice, my voice, *our voice.* Focus, but don't over complicate it, it's easy.

Focus, don't over complicate it.

She smiles at me, "See, you're getting it." My eyes jolt wide open, I didn't even notice I was speaking. Damn, they should've made this ethereal record button more obvious. I don't want to be hitting that thing when I don't want people to hear me.

A couple laughs and happy conversations pass by before the mood changes to utterly somber. Jayden and I meet gazes, we know there's serious business at hand and that there's less and less time to waste.

"Anna, do you remember the voice that responded to you when you set up your meeting spot?" I asked her.

"Yeah, I thought it was you at first. Who was it?"

I shake my head, "I wish it was." I look over at Jayden, I have no idea how to say this, might as well be blunt. "That was the owner of Dragon Tech Incorporated," I look back at her, "he's an ethereal" She furrows her brows. "Theodore Drakone was the one leading you into the alley, his men were the ones who surrounded you. His plan was to find you so he could kidnap you, Anna. He's out to kill us."

She shakes her head with judgement in her eyes, "Isn't this, like, a phone company we're talking about?"

"Hm," I look over to the kids. They all responded with a gaze that fits their personality, Logan had a cocky, shitty little grin, his eyebrows raised ever so slightly. Rose is timid, showing off a forced smile behind a mild whining. Victoria gave me a devious snarling-like look as she raises one eyebrow, "Kind of," I finally respond. I look back at Anastasia and explain the company, Jayden and my employment with them, how I smuggle machinery to keep empowered species like us underground. How Jayden and Logan's jumping ability, albeit useful, create obvious tracks for them to follow.

The atmosphere around the group becomes tense and awkward, all the relief and amusement that once filled their faces is gone. Jayden is stone faced, the kids are obviously troubled. Anna seems to have some inner thoughts tormenting her as the information buzzes around her, Gavin seems lost.

"And since we're all huddled in one spot now, the disturbance in the atmosphere is going to become pretty apparent soon, even while we're however far below ground we are."

"What the plan, bud?" Gavin asks me; he's been totally quiet up until this point, he's awfully good at listening but he doesn't seem the best at understanding. I shutter, I don't have a plan. Realistically, I've been ready for this whole thing to crumble into pieces.

I look to Jayden, he shakes his head. "We need to stop *him*," he mutters, "as long as the director is alive he's a threat." He jumps to his knees and begins drawing phantom lines in the stone with his finger, "Theodore is the brains and wallet behind this operation. This means not only is he the most valuable asset, but he's probably the most guarded as well. If he loses connection with the rest of the company, we'll have a generous amount of time while they try to recount their loss," he looks up. The only light comes from long, dim lights mounted on the walls but their glare shines in Jayden's eyes, "Drakone needs to be silenced, first."

CHAPTER XIII

OUR DEVIOUS PLOT

The hardest part about planning a complex onslaught is trust in others. Everybody's skills are more than necessary but I wouldn't bet my life on any of these people. Their abilities are crucial in making a fully-fledged plan, it's pertinent to our survival; yet, half of the people here don't even know *how* to use their natural talents.

Looking around the stone corridor only hurts my faith. Our best chance of survival is in escape, not attack. Why would we face them head on, it's suicide. I can tell the ambience my expression is giving off, my attitude is beginning to rub off on everybody else.

You need to trust us, Mason, she says in my head. Her voice echoes, ringing around in my brain. Rose looks at me, *Just this one time.*

She's always in my head, she's always reading my thoughts. I look at her and shake my head with doubt. She can say it all she wants but I don't trust her and I don't trust anybody here, especially not for a plan so extravagant.

These people are the closest things I've had to family since my days on the streets. Yet, here I am doubting every single one of them. Why can't I decide on what I want? I want to be alone, yet I want my family by my side, don't I? Just like Red was. Not even the other ethereals make me feel better. All that I've been waiting for feels like there was nothing to become of it.

Maybe I'm afraid that I'll kill them, just like I did Red.

Suddenly, Anna grabs my hand and squeezes it. I look at her in surprise but she talks before I can react, "Mason, stop it." She squeezes my hand even tighter, "We've got nothing to worry about when you're around."

I slowly turn my head to her, astounded. Who does she think she is? What does that even *mean*? I'm concerned on how she interrupted my thoughts so accurately. I swear, if she can read minds like Rose…

My anger begins to bubble.

I rip my hand out from under her, drawing the attention of everybody around. An obvious look of disdain and surprise erupts from everybody but Anna; she makes it look like she understands; this only makes me angrier since there's no way she could. Trying to stay cool I keep my volume low, "Don't act like you know anything."

"Mason, she's trying to help you," Victoria snarls at me, "what's your problem?"

"You're my problem," I snap my glare to her. "You've been *all* of my problems, in case that wasn't obvious."

"Whoa, bud," Gavin gestures in, "keep it cool."

I boil even more. I get ready to blindly explode but Anna's grip catches my attention, I can feel myself bargaining my endurance to my hand completely subconsciously, she's squeezing it with an iron grip. If it weren't for my endurance, this would actually hurt. She looks out to the group as if she's speaking for her child, "Don't worry. Mason doesn't know how to deal with his emotions just yet."

I get ready to scream but she pops me a look I've never witnessed before. Her eyes begin to intensify so much that I can't even focus, my brain feels like it's melting. Her grip hurts now, my head hurts, my chest feels tight. I feel the room spinning, suddenly I'm confused and terrified. The only thing in the room is Anna and me, everybody else begins to wash away like wet paint falling off a canvas. Even the room around me is warping away.

Anna looks at me with death in her eyes as the background turns black, her words have rich echoes, "Mason, listen to me." I can't move, my limbs aren't responding, not even my lungs are acknowledging me. Something is making me breathe and it isn't me. "We don't have any space for error. Play your part, Mason, you're the most important piece."

Is this part of her power? I don't know what kind of ethereal she is. I'm horrified down to my core, I don't understand what's going on, this feels like an actual dream. Without my consent, my eyelids begin to shut, my vision goes black.

I hear her voice, "Wake up, Mason." The echo is dissipating, leaving only her natural voice, "Wake up, Mason!" My eyes shoot open to see everybody else huddled around Jayden across the corridor, Anna is shaking me. My back is propped up against the wall, Jayden looks over at me as I come to. He gives me a quick nod, "I'll catch you up in a second, Mason."

"What the hell ha-" I start but I'm interrupted.

"Play along," Anna whispers in my ear. My throat tightens, I choke a little bit. Never have I been so frightened by somebody, "Mason, what happened to you? You just... Passed out."

I stare at her blankly for a couple seconds, "I... I'm not sure."

Everybody nods in agreement around Jayden who turns his attention over to me. He walks over to me and crouches down to my level, he's holding a small piece of gridded paper. There's small dots and lines that seem to, based on the layout, represent the roads and guards on Rogue Street, "We need to break into teams. If we stay together we'll be surrounded instantly." He points down at the sheet of paper with three lists of names, "We should have three teams, each with one ethereal and or Rose. We can communicate with each other the best, no distance requirements, no delay, quick and efficient contact."

I calculate his words in my head as I soak in the information. "But he'll hear us," I say. Whenever we speak to each other, Theodore is going to hear us, we can't really get around that.

"That's what we want." Jayden peers down at me, "We can set

it up so we have three groups in three different locations. We'll communicate with each other, via ethereal, about where each party is. They'll go off what we say but the groups will be scrambled, totally different areas than we describe. They'll prepare to launch an attack for the wrong targets on every side."

I'm surprised by his brilliance, his plan is well constructed. Rose walks up with her hands tightly held behind her back, "We all have pretty obvious strengths and weaknesses. We need to think this one out, use that against them." I look at her puzzled, she's gotten much more outspoken.

This was Rose's plan, wasn't it?

Piece by piece, the puzzle built itself into the beautiful, dangerous portrait of a plan ready to execute. There's a lot of us, a lot at stake here, a lot of pressure on our shoulders. I need to keep myself composed, keep my stance poised, keep my mind in check. I know that we're all ready to do this.

Right? I'm ready, aren't I?

Anna's booming voice vividly repeats in my head. She did something to me, she said I'm the most important piece. She sounds like she knows so much but I don't understand why she would.

Okay. Anna, Victoria, and Rose, you guys make your way to the off of 2nd and Rogue Street. Gavin, Logan, and Jayden, you guys make your way farther up North a couple blocks and wait at the bus stop, you guys will have to be our bait. Veronica and I will be East about three blocks on Red Street.

In my head, I can hear two repeating sentences, *Got it*. Running into our positions, everybody gets in place and sets up. Jayden said he was able to use the built in radar from his company phone, he should be able to make sure he sees what we see.

Jayden says we're all clear, their eyes are our eyes.

Our troops were placed. As far as they know we're within matching weaknesses, Victoria, Rose, and Anna are all smart and tactical but have little physical strength or speed advantage. Gavin, Logan, and Jayden are our quick maneuvers, swift, the hardest to catch but easiest to contain. They can skip from place to place with immense speed but once they get figured out their motions become abstract. Veronica and I have similar abilities, using our talents to change the way we fight. The easiest way to get through us is by exhausting us.

The company has all hands on deck this time, once they see there's so many of us, they're going to throw everything on the table. Be prepared. On the count of three, send up your signals. One...

I steady my mind, put myself in a stance of focus and concentration. I need to use my abilities in a way that's obvious, something easy to catch on a radar.

Two...

Two others should be preparing to do the same thing, we're all playing bait.

Three!

This is it. As fast as I can I drain and consume my power, recode my soul over and over again in every way I can think of, most of it senseless, of no purpose. Multiple bargains at once, every single one I conjure up without destroying my energy storage. All I'm doing is sending out a flare.

Jayden says that radar is off the charts, they should be here any minute.

Minutes away, the tension builds in my chest. It feels like a soda bottle ready to explode, as if there's a pressure in my throat getting tighter and tighter, I'm starting to sweat. It falls ominously quiet; I don't hear a footstep, an attack, not even breathing. I feel like somebody's watching, waiting.

We've got one! We're running!

That's a lie, that was Anna. We're throwing them off. The more in the dark they are, the less they know, the easier it'll be for us to have the upper hand. They should be coming any second but I don't see a thing.

I hear a screech.

Far out in the distance I hear wheels squealing in agony, vehicles skidding around the block corner. I hide behind the alley wall, they're going to be pretty surprised when they figure out that I'm totally alone.

I'm on the alley on 2nd and Rogue Street. If our plan worked like it was supposed to, they should be coming here prepared for Victoria, Rose, and Anna. Those three are all at a physical disadvantage whereas physicality is my biggest strength.

Screeching to a stop, two black SUV's block the street in front of me. Flooding out came three men per vehicle, each equipped with either a stun rod or a neck trap, a long rod with a metal rope on the end laced into an adjustable noose. They're ready for minimal combat and quick capture but they have no idea who they're up against.

I take a single step as powerful as I can, the concrete below my toes cracks with the pressure. I fly forward out of the alley, they can't keep up with my speed. Stunned by the new target they stumble around. The men in suits begin to pool up, I start picking them off.

Dashing in towards the crowd, I dish out punches and elbows to each one I can. The most difficult part of combat for me is timing; I can only be proficient on a handful of things at once. I'm slow when I'm strong, weak when I'm quick. I needed to stay tactical and flexible, I needed to keep an eye on everybody at once.

I throw my elbow into a woman's nose and quickly drop my head. A stun rod swings right over my head, I bring my foot around, a shorter man goes tumbling to the ground. Grabbing the woman by the collar and pants pocket, I lob her into two of the others packed tightly together; clumsily, they begin to attack each other, misfiring their weapons and striking their allies. The stun rod makes contact with another's neck, he spasms out of control. They were extremely ill prepared for this fight, they expected kids with low endurance to fall right into their hands. One by one, like chess pieces, they begin to fall.

I drop my body, my knees bend and my back arches so far that the back of my head touches the ground. A pair of wires flies out above me, I can smell the static electricity radiating off of the chords, they gleam in the sunlight. They latch into another guard's chest. I drop my hands on the ground by my head and pull my feet up, kicking my body into the air. Rotating as I fall down, I use the back of my shoe to kick the wires away, knocking the weapon out of its owner's hands and relieving the shock from the other.

Focusing in harder and harder, I keep myself moving, keep my body warm as I fight. I'm at a flanking disadvantage; I'm not scared of any single strike but if my attention gets averted then I'm left open to another. Small attacks add up quickly. Two get up, four remain on their feet; three, two. I'm in my element.

When I was in the underground ring, I never fought more than one person at a time. When I was on the streets, I fought large groups pretty often when they thought I'd be an easy target for robbing.

I'm not.

Before I can take another deep breath, every suited guard is lying on the ground in small piles. I don't know how long they'll be out but they're not my main threat, they're in a good enough position for me.

I search the body of each one pulling out wires and devices, crushing each one beneath my feet and between my fingers. Satisfied by my search, I take a step forward to make my way down the road but I'm interrupted, I catch a flailing metal rope out of the corner of my eyes. I let my guard down too quick.

Too late to react, I feel a tight string brace itself around my throat; I start suffocating, I can't breath. I gasp and wail for air but I'm not getting any. I wrap my hands around the lace in an attempt to pull it off but it's only getting tighter. Another door opens. From one of the SUV's, I see the feet of Mr. Parker, his well-tailored suit, darkest colored clothing of all the men, his freshly polished shoes shining in the sun. A pair of sunglasses prevents me from seeing his eyes, I can tell that this man is ready to kill me. His glare is hiding something, something sinister.

Approaching slowly, he swiftly grabs one of the stun rods from the incapacitated men. He presses the button over and over, fiddling with the trigger like a toy; I didn't plan to get contained yet. I can only stay awake for so much longer, if they subdue me I'll be a goner. I won't be able to escape like this.

Somebody is holding the lace, I can see somebody on the ground with the extended shaft of a neck trap in their hands, yet I can't see who it is. I can't even rotate my body, something is stopping me.

Think; I can't think, I'm not getting enough air to think. The rope cinches tighter around my neck. Looking back I can see his stone cold face. His sick, twisted grimace snarling at me as I struggle. I could pull forward, I could try to grab it, take it from his hands; I can't breathe, all I can think about is how I can't breathe. I need air. I need air *now*.

My vision begins to blur but I can see him approaching, his figure is obscure. He thrusts the rod at me, bright blue electricity arcs down its shaft. I brace for pain but I don't feel anything, I feel fine. In fact, I can breathe again. The noose loosens away from my neck.

I watch in astoundment as Mr. Parker electrocutes the man holding my noose, over and over, poking and prodding at him as he squirms in pain. He's struggling like a bug drowning in a drop of water. Mr. Parker shoots me a glare; he reaches into his pocket and pulls out a ring of keys. Tossing them at me I hear a familiar, odd-for-his-appearance feminine voice, "Let's go."

He lifts up his sunglasses to reveal a bright pair of violet eyes. She winks at me.

CHAPTER XIV

HAND AND HAND, A MAN FOR A MAN

I vividly remember a time with the company when we found a surreal, when Dragon Tech captured somebody in front of me. No more than months ago; I never figured out what his powers were but he was pretty damn strong. We sent our men for weeks in waves to find him, small guys to special operation managers, man after man, he always prevailed even though he was totally alone.

After so much fighting they finally arrested him. I was in the building when I saw him get dragged in; a steel noose was tightened around his neck, his hands and legs bound together, guards were constantly following behind him, shocking him when he struggled. We met gazes, fear and agony in his expression, dry blood mats his hair to his face. Electrocuted again, he wailed out in pain. He gave up, I could see it in his eyes. He's stopped fighting. He could get out again if he wanted but what would happen? It was a stalemate, he'd get away, they'd send more; the cycle was perpetual, never ending. He'd be trying to escape for the rest of his life and he'd rather just get caught then keep running forever.

He was thrown in a small cell, no bed, no sunlight, nothing of comfort. I visited him any chance I got, talked to him, smuggled in food for him. I'd ask him what he wanted so I could go out and grab it. It was always Thai, he loved Thai food.

I didn't want him contained. if I had a say in the matter, he would've been liberated. It wasn't my call, though, it wasn't my choice whether he stays or goes. I didn't even have access to open the cell.

I could've broken him out but nothing would have changed.

Every day they would escort him out of his cell to run experiments on him. I hated to hear it but I listened to him about every single one he went through; stabbing, prodding, poking, draining; anything they could've done, they did. I saw his skin grow pale, I saw hair fall off his scalp over time. The stress was getting to him, he was tortured for so long. They didn't care what they did to him, they didn't care for him at all. They cared about what made him tick, what granted him power.

"I'm getting out next time, Mason," he told me, sitting curled up in the corner of his cell. "I'm escaping," he paused to cough up a clot of blood, "or I'm dying on the way out." I hated to hear him say it, he had been tortured to his breaking point. I know why he wanted it but I hated to see him want it.

His skin began to sink in, his hips and shoulders protruded beneath his skin. When I asked him what he wanted to eat he'd ignore me. After a while, he stopped eating all together.

"How can I help you?" I asked. I was so worried, I wanted him out of here, I wanted him to be free, I wanted him gone. With the skin under his eyes dark and sagging he looked up at me, peering through me, "I'll want a distraction."

Days later I walked up to the story above, I could see his cell below me. There's a long walkway above the first floor leading to a large metal platform. To the beat of his command I waited for his signal. The guards walked up to open his cell, each equipped with oppressive weaponry. Not this time; I watched as they typed in the code. Walking to the platform I saw that nobody was present, it was totally vacant there.

He typed in the code. I could hear it beeping upon every number. I was getting nervous; I waited and watched.

He looks at me.

I thrashed my arms around sending one of the machines flying. In front of me was a table full of contraptions, mechanical devices, things far beyond my realm of knowledge. I've seen laboratory workers tinker with these plenty of times, but more importantly, I've heard them tell me not to touch them. Some very specific machines, in fact. I threw one across the room by accident.

The machine began clapping against itself, a hinge holding two pieces of metal apart; it went haywire. Chewing like an alligator jaw, it flailed around, gnawing on the other machines. I have no idea what purpose that machine served other than the perfect cause of a distraction.

Metal was clinking, glasses fell on the ground shattering, "What the hell is going on!?" I cried out, "These machines are going insane!" My booming voice threw the guards spinning to see what's going on, the clapping machine lead its destruction over the edge, falling off the platform and onto the floor below. The guards attempted to run up and grab the machine but its metal jaws chomped on their arms. Crying out in pain, the other guards struggled to try to halt it with the nooses they had in hand. Catching it like a necrotic butterfly in a steel net, he tightened the grip on the trap enough to suppress its biting. Together, the guards fought to restrain it while scientists flooded in frantically, freaking out and screaming about their lovely contraptions, how much work it took to build them, how much it'll cost to rebuild them. All the things I'm sure the guards weren't thinking.

Little did anybody know, the cell was open the whole time. Machines were still falling from the top platform, glass was still shattering, machines were still exploding. His chance to escape had become openly apparent. I didn't even see him any more, he should have been gone by now.

BOOM!

The sound echoed through the halls, I had no idea where it came from. I'd been making noise the whole time but that was way louder than anything that'd happened thus far; it had everybody's attention.

I looked over as I watched his lifeless body drop to the ground, totally limp. A bullet wound entombed itself in his chest, he didn't even squirm. Blood drained from his shirt; his carcass falling revealed the assassin standing amongst us all. Mr. Parker took a stance there, a gun pointed at where the surreal used to be, where he would be standing if he was still alive. Captured, tortured, and finally shot from point blank.

I take the keys and ignite the engine. Rose appears in the seat next to me as she disengages her invisibility. Right now, more commotion is what we want; attention puts them at a disadvantage, they can't let people know what's going on, nobody knows about the empowered species, nobody knows the truth. The public knowing the truth would put this company underground given they avoid being condemned completely.

We purposely chose locations towards the outskirts of the barricades. The noise we make will not only force the guards to be less reactive due to the public eye but people will also begin to notice if we play our cards right.

Driving North up Rogue Street we see the remains of another battle taking place. Little bustle is happening at this point, Victoria and Anna have already made good work of their opponents. The spot where Logan, Jayden, and Gavin should've been, Victoria and Anna stand triumphant as they finish off the last of the men. Equipped with electric-resistance equipment and paper-thin clothing, Anna and Victoria were easily able to take them on; their armor was made to stop electricity, not flying acid bullets and…. Whatever Anna does.

Jumping out of the SUV, I throw the keys to Anna. Switching spots with me, Anna jumps in while I jump out. Clumsily, Anna makes her way to the final location where Gavin and Logan stand, leaving just Victoria and I.

Everybody stay in position, I'm sure more are on their way!

Letting everybody know that we're supposed to be staying in our original position, we scramble the teams again. Jayden has been hiding this whole time underground but now he gets to show his face. Veronica will be with the last group soon enough, she's taken another vehicle herself, she should be on her way. Once the last group gets their SUV, they'll make their way back to Rogue Street, right back where we started.

Reinforcements should be coming any minute, probably equipped with lethal weaponry. We need to keep on switching up the parties, take on the offhand agents until the director decides to show his face.

The three groups have been blended. Up North is Victoria and I, Jayden approaching as soon as more men show up. He'll be staying low so he can catch them off guard. East of Rogue Street is Anna and Rose, Veronica will be sneaking up disguised; she's a crucial part of the end goal. Logan and Gavin should be driving down to our beginning center position at any moment; Dragon Tech reinforcements should be on their way.

Don't think for a moment that you have us fooled. You're not going anywhere, we're not falling for your dainty little tricks.

His voice may be the same voice I've heard so many times but this time it sends a shiver down my spine.

This was over the moment you began resisting.

Finally he decides to reveal himself. The bond that holds us together stronger than blood, he's using it to aid his threats. Us ethereals have the potential of so much power. Working together comes like second nature to us, why would he try so hard to ruin this? He's ruining everything *we* could've had.

I hear blades chop at the air above us, loud whooshing noises curl away the wind; a chopper. Where the hell did they get a helicopter? Rushing towards the sky directly above us, the aircraft waves its ugly head about a hundred feet up. Something's inside it, something huge, something dark. I can't make out its shape.

That is, at least, until it's tumbling straight towards us.

CHAPTER XV

REAL METAL, REAL PAIN

The figure was humanoid; dark tinted glass and bright colored metal shimmered in the sun, its glare climbing up its body as it descended to us. It must be at least twelve feet tall in its crouched position, the robotic monstrosity makes a deadly landing to the concrete, craters left where its feet made contact. Rock shrapnel flies towards us, Victoria yelps as she shields us with a wall of shadowy material.

I've seen this before.

These aren't robots, they're suits; there's somebody piloting them, I can make out a human silhouette in the tinted glass. Guns, weapons, tools of destruction are sprinkled all over the mech. I'm sure all the little slits and squares will reveal more when the time comes.

Mason, Gavin, the director is piloting the South robot, I can tell; when he speaks it's coming from that one. That's got to be him.

Rocketing through the air, I see a huge fist fly at us at unfathomable speed, reflexively I grab Victoria and roll out of the way; the radius of catastrophe still makes it to us. The giant steel fist creates a gigantic crater, a seismic wave destroys a large radius of asphalt around it. These men must be insane. They're destroying so much, I can't imagine they're still trying to keep it a secret. It's bad enough to destroy the city, but to spend millions upon millions of dollars on machinery like this? What do they *really* want?

I look to Victoria as I release her, "We need to run!" Our skin is bruised and damaged, blood trickles from open wounds on us both. She can't run as fast as I can but I don't know how far or how fast I can run carrying her. On top of that, I have no idea how fast that giant mech can go, either. Maybe we can take the car.

Suddenly, a subtle flash of light sparks next to me, Jayden appears. Jumping in surprise, Victoria attempts to run back but I grab her arm before she can. Looking at me with disdain she tries to fight out of reaction; Jayden's too quick. Together, all three of us disappear and reappear a hundred feet down the road, barely dodging another attack. Another fist reigns down where we used to stand. We start running.

Making a break South, Victoria and Jayden follow me; I have to keep to a slower pace for them to keep up with me. Behind us, I can see the giant robot freak spin around towards us, I doubt it can run fast enough to catch up to us now.

That is, unless of course, it had rockets or something.

Flames begin to spew from the back of the automation. With one giant leap it closes half of the distance between us. Falling into a run, the mech attempts to stay on us by foot; it'll never catch up. It boosts fast but runs slow. I hear another spark fire from it. With quick reaction, Jayden suddenly grabs both of us before getting totally squashed by the huge hunk of steel. A hundred feet farther, I can see the others trying to handle their mech as well. A hundred feet forward and we'll be helping.

I look over to Jayden as we run, "These things are huge, it should be pretty hard for them to fight side by side."

Without removing his gaze from the fight happening in front of us he speaks, "Then let's get them all together."

Running into the heat of battle, we meet Gavin and Logan; they're alive but they don't seem like they're doing too well. Gavin can't bring company when he transitions between planes, if that robot chooses to target Logan, he won't have any means of escape. At the moment, the mech is tossing and turning trying to find a good grip on the Plane Walker.

"Jayden, take Victoria out for a second," I yell. It's getting harder and harder to hear anything over the deafening noise of battle. I pick up my speed towards the robot, *my* full sprint. Jayden disappears with Victoria as the mech behind us begins to gain on me. Leap by leap, it makes its way until...

WHAM!

Sliding underneath the legs of the one in front of me, the two giant machines collide, sending them both flying, tumbling around the streets; rolling over cars and knocking down poles and signs. Flying balls of fire and destruction.

Anna, meet us at the center point. We're getting the family all together.

Anna, Rose, and Veronica are going to have a hard time taking on the mech by themselves. Rose isn't strong enough to handle herself in a situation, if she doesn't find a way to deal with her timid nature quickly, she'll be a goner. Veronica will be more than able to fend for herself, transforming into another person is good for disguising, but transforming into something as small as a rat or squirrel is *really* good for hiding.

I don't know what Anna does but I can't imagine her having too much of a problem.

Stumbling to their feet, both machines begin their pursuit of us again. The dark metal has lost its luster, chips of paint and scraps of metal are bitten out of each machine but their limbs seem to function just fine. The large glass canopies covering the pilots have huge cracks where they collided but they're not in pieces yet.

Jayden starts zapping around; he's pulling the attention of one of them. He can't do it forever, but the little he can do will be a great distraction to keep them off of us. Attempting to do the same, Gavin begins to change his position sporadically, appearing and disappearing from reality over and over again but the second mech isn't phased. It's got its eyes set on target, its charge doesn't falter. I know what he's looking at, he's looking at me. It's my director, he's taking me on first, he's trying to take me *out* first.

Distracted by combat, the others begin taking on the mech who's spinning in confusion from Jayden's light show. Logan and Victoria work together to launch electro-acid attacks from afar. Gavin is trying to get the automation to waiver but he's too keen on taking me down. Before I know it, Gavin is too far away to help and I've got one right on my tail. Quick to change my stance, I try to move out of the way in order to keep myself from getting flattened. This thing may have me on size but it has nothing on me for dexterity.

I'm stopped by something. A metal coil wraps itself around my legs and body, I topple over. Looking up, I see my director's machine has halted, staying in position. He doesn't plan to run me over, he plans to bring me to him. The chain begins to retreat into the arm of the machine dragging me in. Squirming and struggling, I see that I'm too tightly wound; this chain was made to hold a person in confinement, to fish somebody out. Gavin, even with his abilities, can only reach me at running speed at best. There's not enough time, I'm getting roped in fast.

This feels like the ethereal rope. Tugging me, pulling me, forcing me in. They hurt just the same.

Finally in fingertip's reach, the robot picks me up, crushing me with its grip. I'm suffocating, I can't breath, I can't raise my chest enough to get air. My ribs and the bones in my chest are breaking and fracturing; I feel them, I *hear* them. I'm nothing compared to the death grip this machine has on me, I can't move, I have no air.

I've been waiting, Mason. I've been waiting for you.

I look deep into the dark, cloudy glass. I search for my director's icy glare, his evil eyes and deathly, smug grimace. If I'm not going to make it out I might as well get one last good look. I bargain to the best of my limited ability, my vision becomes fierce, any better and I could see through walls.

I peer into the dark window but I don't see Theodore. My director isn't piloting this machine but I know for a fact that this machine is where that voice came from. I *know* our voice came from this automation's pilot.

It's not my director, it's Mr. Parker.

CHAPTER XVI

THE JESTER
BEHIND THE TRICKS

Mr. Parker is an ethereal, just like us. This old, cruel, heartless fiend has been apart of our brotherhood this whole time; our lifelong bond as those who've been together since the beginning. A bond so strong, yet he breaks is as he attempts to kill me, one of his own.

His grip grows even tighter; I can't make it at this rate.

Not this time, Mason. This time, there will be no foil. Genius like this can't be stopped!

My vision blurs, I can't think straight anymore, I can't see straight anymore. The pain is unbearable. I need air that I'm not getting. It feels like I should fall asleep. We're so close, yet I'm sitting trapped in arrest, just out of reach. I can feel my life spilling out of my pores.

I fall.

His grip has completely loosened. I gasp for air, filling my body with all that I can get. I attempt to reinflate my shrivelled lungs. I crave air. My ribs are definitely broken, pain stabs my sides.

I look up, a large steel rod has been inserted into the arm of the machine like a titan's flu shot, static begins to spark around the injection point. As the arm begins to flail uncontrollably, Mr. Parker's machine pulls it out like a toothpick, tossing it to the side.

What?

Looking around, I see nobody, sense nobody, I can't even smell anybody. Gavin stands beside me, he's at my aid. If it wasn't him, who could it be? Rose, maybe she's here; no, I'd hear her with my heightened senses, smell her even. I look around again. I do smell *something...*

Standing in front of me are a boy and a girl, both facing the tanking robot. Their bodies are shaped similarly besides their masculine versus feminine features, their hair the same color. They must be siblings. They're not familiar at all, I don't recognize either of them. They both have shimmering black hair and caramel skin, their height difference only inches.

I feel slightly magnetized towards them, subtly pulled in by them. They're both half-ethereals.

Standing before me are Flickerers, a breed of ethereals imbued with the ability to do what reality deemed impossible: altering, creating, and destroying matter. The complexity of their power is far beyond anything I understand but I do know that they can create objects from nothing for short increments of time. Like nothing even happened, it will destroy itself without a trace. Great consequence and great power comes from abilities like these, both being way above my pay grade.

Turning back to look at me, the two kids offer me a hand. How did they get here? *Why* did they get here?

They must've heard us.

Over all this time, Anna has been shooting messages to the entire species, giving our location, creating meeting plans, constantly updating the others on where we were. Although they were meant for one person they ended up being heard by every ethereal in existence. Maybe they're driven the same way I was, the same way Anna was. They want to meet the others, see who has been tugging at us relentlessly for so long. They wanted to solidify the connection we had, to listen to the voiceless.

Both of their faces are soft but mature, their matching outfits include a black t-shirt and light brown, skinny pants. The girl's hair is long and sleek, the boy's hair is short and messy, swiped partially to one side.

I take the hand they offer me, together they help me up. No words get exchanged, rather, stances are taken and we prepare. In the distance, one machine topples over in a failed attempt to catch Jayden. Together, Logan and his brother instill immense current into the machine; it seizures up, flailing its limbs uncontrollably.

Closer to us, Mr. Parker has got his machine back on his feet; his severed arm is malfunctioning, squirming around, occasionally even damaging the mech. Rather than fret over it he boosts himself into the air. I watch as he plummets down to us, I run out of his path of destruction in an attempt to distance myself as much as possible. Looking back, I see the other two trying to make way for the machine but they're not fast enough. Just between them the machine crashes, waves of destruction send the two flying in opposite directions. The impact renders the boy unconscious, the girl rolls over in agony, blood matted on her face where her forehead has opened.

I can't take this anymore. I'm taking this freak on, one on one. No more running away; I can feel myself being drawn in by him, lead by an invisible rope. Mr. Parker's plan is to kill us all, eradicate his own species. The rope he pulls me with is wrapped around my neck and I'm sick of it.

Jumping from side to side, I make my way towards him as fast as I can. He punches the ground but I use the force it makes to propel myself. Hitting the wall, I put as much force and energy into my legs as possible and jump to the machine's face; the glass casing that holds him. I can't find a grip, it's slippery, smooth, nowhere to grab. Slowly sliding off, I find a foothold below the glass casing, a small opening right where the glass and metal meet, just enough to get my toes in.

The machine's flailing arm begins to swat at me, I can't dodge it unless I leap off the machine. Looking back, I watch at least a metric ton of steel drive its way into my spine, the pain renders me immobile for a moment, my grip suddenly becoming weaker, my bones feel like they've shattered; it's possible they did. Looking in front of me, my body has created an indent in the glass, a spiderweb-style crack has encased itself in the robot's face plate. My body is bleeding, it hurts all over. The sting is pulsating, I'm in so much pain.

I don't allow it to sway me, I'm ending this here and now. I take a leap up, make my way to the top. The only thing to grab is a crack in the glass, a small hole where the glass flew out. Gripping it, I can feel it slicing into my palm. I *refuse* to let go. Parker tries to fend me off, he flails his working hand above my head in failed attempts. Ducking my head, I let his strikes freefly; he's not getting me off, I won't let him.

Looking down below the giant steel body, I see Gavin has carried the Flickerers together, he's taking them far away from the wreckage.

The malfunctioning arm makes one damaging squirm before Parker finally kicks it high up into the wall of a skyscraper, shattering the glass and sending it into a once-tidy office space. Its strike destroys the building from the inside out, glass and rock crumbles down as it digs its way through the stories. The ground isn't able to hold its weight, especially while it's thrashing After seconds, sparks fly as the severed arm slowly loses all its motivation, it goes limp as it loses its life. Mr. Parker is angry, his judgement is impaired, he's sick of me and I'm glad.

The limb, in its last bit of life, crawls its way out of buildings. Slowly rocking on the edge of the third story of the building, it finally plummets down.

I watch as the several-ton arm hurtles towards Gavin and the others, right where they are lying. I don't have time to react, I can't reach them from here; they won't survive that impact if I don't do *something*.

But I'm too far away.

CHAPTER XVII

A CALL FROM NO REALITY

I watch in terror, helpless. Just a moment ago, I fought on, I frothed at the mouth just thinking about the power and strength I was using. I was fearless. Pain, restraint, obstruction, none of it slowed me down, I was here until my job was completed. I wouldn't take dying for an answer, I was finishing my task. I was going to end this cruel robot's life, I was going to end this cruel man's reign.

Now I'm helpless, I'm afraid. Absolutely terrified. I can't do anything, I can't even move. I'm petrified, my muscles won't respond. The three who saved my life today, they're in danger and I can't return the favor. If nobody does anything, they'll die.

I can't do anything.

The arm descends towards the half-ethereals; Gavin stands up. Sticking his hands in the air, he closes his eyes and braces himself. The arm doesn't go through them all, it disappears; in the blink of an eye, Gavin and the arm are gone. It didn't drag Gavin down, Gavin dragged it down.

Even though Gavin can't take visitors when he transitions from plane to plane, he can bring objects. He brought the arm with him so it wouldn't kill all three of them, he carried it to another plane where it would only kill one. He couldn't stop the velocity, he couldn't stop the sheer speed it was moving at but he could save the others.

War suddenly falls silent, I can't hear anything. My ears are ringing. I pause, sit in silence as I try to comprehend what just happened, what I just experienced. Parker stands beneath me, placed in his wreckage, nothing but murder in his eyes. He doesn't even speak for his regret, he didn't even give Gavin a chance to say a word before his life was ended; a heroic show of courage, quick wits; *he's dead now.* I can't stand it, I can't take anymore. I can't even begin to fathom how I feel; but I can feel it in my heart.

I have a strong connection with all ethereals, within and outside of reality. I can feel the life essence of every single ethereal alive. Slowly, I can sense it within myself; one life force, one of the few of us fades away. Slowly, our connection is broken as his life is drained from him. No more pulling, no more connection, nothing more from Gavin.

Turning my attention back to the glass, the casing I'm hanging on, I straighten out and cock back. More than I've ever done before, I'm leaving myself completely and utterly vulnerable, I'm leaving myself with two strengths: the muscles in my arm and the grip in my hand. My speed is turned to nothing, my senses are drained completely; my conscience is gone.

Screaming in anger, I begin to hit the glass with my bare fist. Blow after blow, I release everything I have unto it; not just my fists, not just my anger, *all* of me. I let nothing to waste as I reveal this wretched man, relieve him of his weaponry. It starts to crack, more and more, I can almost see him inside it.

Jab after jab, I watch red spew from my fingers. Broken glass and metal shrapnel relieves me of my blood, relieves me of my life force; I don't need it. Pain won't contain me, *pain won't bring Gavin back.*

A quick jolt brings us both forwards, he's trying to run but he won't get me off. I don't look up, I don't move my gaze. If I would have, I would've known that I wasn't the reason he ran.

Another hit. Another hit.

My grip is taken from me when another tower of steel crashes into the one I'm on. I'm sent flailing through the air, I don't have enough time to fully regain my endurance before I hit the wall behind me. I can't move now, I'm tumbling to the ground, I'm a dozen feet in the air, I'm pretty sure every bone in my body is in two or more pieces, this fall won't be healthy for me.

Below me, something begins to fade into existence. Climbing towards me as I plummet, I fall onto a large pile of fine sand about six feet below, cushioning my fall and dispersing below me as I reach it. Lying in pain, I can feel it disappear below me until I'm lying on the ground, unable to move. The girl, the Flickerer, drops her hand with fatigue, her abilities draining her of what little energy she had left.

Parker's mech tumbles to the side, the impact of the third machine has completely shattered its glass. Mr. Parker is totally open, he's completely vulnerable. The machine can no longer protect him, he's fallen unconscious inside it. The machine lies on its side, totally motionless, as its pilot hangs by his seatbelt off the side of the chair. Every control, every wire inside, every button is exposed. *He's* exposed.

Fury fills my body; I make myself get to my knees, get to my feet, get myself together. The pain is agonizing. The aching, the stabbing feeling, the feeling of being tied in a knot and hit over and over and over again. My skin is shredded, my blood oozing out of my body faster and faster; the majority of my body is darkened by bruising, tears fall from my eyes as I try to walk away. I'm not letting this stop me, I'm not letting *anything* stop me.

"Mason, *don't!*" she screams. Rose cries out, trying to pull me back with her voice as she runs towards me. I can feel her telekinetic abilities trying to hold me back; she can't. I have to do this, I need to finish him off, I need to end this here and now. I march my way towards him, nothing but blind fury in my eyes, white-hot fire and agony.

I make my final step before I get ready to take stance and deal a final blow but he's faster than me. He wasn't asleep, he was awake the whole time; he was waiting. Rose knew that, she tried to warn me. Out of nowhere, his hand grips the controls and sends the levers flying, the single arm it has responds by swiping at me, sending me spiraling through the air.

I hit the ground, tumbling, rolling, bouncing away like I'm lifeless. I can't stop myself, I just keep crashing and flailing; every time I hit the ground pain surges through my body. I can't let it stop me.

But I can't get up. Not at all. My body won't listen.

I lie on the sidelines, the asphalt oddly comfortable, almost enough to fall asleep. My vision blurs, not from pain but from tears. I can't help but feel sad, angry; my emotions begin to flood over me. In the distance I now see a battle of three mechanized monsters, dishing out, fighting, beating up all my friends; getting beaten up by all my friends.

Rose runs to my side. She drops to her knees, tears rushing down her face. She tries to choke up words but she can't, she's scared and sad as usual; except this time I understand it. She can't help me, she can't fight, she needs to leave me. She needs to bring her friends aid, the ones in battle. If I'm a goner then so be it, don't waste several lives to try to save mine, she knows she has to leave me. She knows that she's a necessity in this battle, she needs to be there.

I can feel her refusing, I can feel her arguing in my head, she's trying to disagree. She's reading my thoughts and showing me hers, she wants to stay, she wants to sit here by my side; she can't. Go, Rose. *Go. Leave!*

Sobbing in rage and anguish, she rests her head on my chest. My body is caked in blood, my jacket is tattered and ripped. She gets up, grabbing my hand. She squeezes it; it hurts but it's comforting. I'm sorry, Rose. I wish I could finish this myself.

Don't give up, Mason.

Anna. I don't know how she heard, I don't know how she knows what I'm feeling. Maybe I accidentally told everybody what I was thinking. I don't care, whatever happened doesn't matter. I wish I could apologize to them all; I'm sorry I couldn't finish this. I'm sorry I'm so damn useless.

Rose wipes away her tears helplessly but they cascade down. She gets up and shoots me a brave and terrified glare, in my mind I can hear her as she runs away, into the battle, *I love you, Mason.*

These goddamn kids.

CHAPTER XVIII

THE REAL STORY

When I was 8 years old, I killed my best friend.

Living in an orphanage in California, I was an outcast, treated like garbage, rarely fed, commonly bullied. I was a scrawny child, kids often enjoyed beating my guts in. Only one person got me through it all; Alice Weston, the happiest girl I've ever met.

Her hair was long and illuminating, it was so bright it almost seemed white. At the ends of each loch it would lightly curl, her bangs were usually wrapped back and clipped. Her eyes were vibrant, colored like the ocean; her nose and cheeks were porcelain. Every feature she had was beautiful, I'll never forget what she looked like when she smiled.

When I was young, I frequently used my powers without realizing. This is dangerous given what I do; I became very ill many times, prone to disease, prone to injury from the way I'd accidentally bargain away my endurance. It took many years for me to get a grip on what I was doing and how to control it. Nobody knew about it but Alice.

Alice helped me learn how to control it. We would go outside and play with the souls of the animals and critters that scurried around.

When I was young, it didn't seem like much. Looking back now I was probably torturing them. Although, the things I learned were crucial to harnessing my abilities as a Striker.

The orphanage we lived in was huge, very rich and preppy. From what I learned, kids from lower social statuses got cast away as scum; my parents were probably povertous, whoever the bastards were. Often, the staff wouldn't allow me to go where all the other kids were allowed to go but I was able to sneak around pretty easily. Alice helped a lot, her family was much wealthier than mine so she got in easy.

One of my favorite places to go with her was the library. A lot of fiction books reminded me of myself; big heroes with strong powers that they hadn't harnessed until the end of the story. Alice would always read them to me since she did it much better than I could.

"He leapt from the heavens with her in his arms," she read. "Their souls mixed as they de-de-scen-ded, love and power they shared." The story of Zandilar, Hero of the Skies. "Like the wind through leaves, their hearts and essence in-ter-t-twined," she'd stutter as she tried to read, "they shared themselves as those who would never depart."

I never really understood the story but it was my absolute favorite, mostly because she liked it so much. I loved the way she smiled when she read it to me. Something about the idea of intertwining souls made her so happy, so giddy inside. She found it so romantic.

I thought maybe I could try.

In the midst of the sunrise we sat in the field out the back of the orphanage, skipping out on class. I never got in trouble for it, the teachers never cared about where I was. For her, though, this was risky.

I grabbed her hands gently, our fingers were so young and untarnished. I was so much paler, so much younger, so naive.

I focused a bargain on the both of us. Mixing our souls together, rotating them, mixing them each into two halves of the same. I could feel them swirling, mixing, combining together. It was peaceful, it felt so benign; like I was closer to her than anybody I had ever known before.

It hurt so bad.

After mere seconds, as if I was getting bucked off my steed, I lost control. I lost my grip on my actions and we began to suffer. I was funneling myself quickly into her and vise versa, over and over, painfully destroying our bodies.

As an ethereal, I had a much easier time surviving this. This may have been harsh but the aether, where souls exist, was my home. She wasn't so lucky, so durable.

The worst part of it all was watching her writhe. When it was happening she was screaming; when it was all over, she was limp with a grimace etched in her lips. Never had I seen a single of her tears, much less watch her cry out in agony.

I'm tarnsihed with the fear of murder, so scared of the meaning of taking a life. Innocent or evil, a life is a life and it's not mine to control. I can't kill a man, I don't have it in me. It's not my place to choose who lives or dies.

I still keep a small bit of her soul to this day. Sometimes I think it's the only reason I can still feel happy.

I'm falling in and out of consciousness; if I fall asleep for too long I may not wake up again. Honestly, it doesn't sound too bad right now. Taking a nice long dirt nap sounds pleasant. Maybe my emotions are playing with me, maybe my brain is losing the blood it needs, maybe I'm crazy. I know I want to sleep; it's awfully comfy here.

Through my interrupted consciousness I see a pair of feet, a familiar pair of feet. Nice shoes, smooth and shiny, black like the pants he's wearing. His slacks look freshly ironed even though blood stains them. He has a limp, a coagulated circle of blood builds on his left thigh; it looks like a bullet wound. His clothes are familiar, his skin is familiar; even his body shape is familiar.

His icy glare is too familiar.

He limps towards me, it seems his frigid expression has been wiped off his face. My director makes his way to me in pain; his suit jacket unbuttoned and tattered, his white shirt stained with an ungodly amount of red, as if somebody spilled a paint bucket on him. His hair has been ruined, I can see a line of blood leaving a red streak on his forehead. Three wounds, was he shot? By who? And why so many times?

Maybe he's here to shoot me.

My mind begins to blend together, all of my thoughts begin buzzing around in my head, almost as blurry as my vision. Thoughts about the battle going on, thoughts about the people who may die today, thoughts about Gavin, about Anna, about Drakone.

Where his cold attitude used to be lies a sad, inexpressive face. Disdain and guilt floods his eyes and lips; I've never seen him with another expression. This look is foreign on him, it doesn't match his body.

"K-kill me, Mason," he says. He's heaving. I take a double take, astonished by his performance. He drops to his knees, his face has a single drop of blood crawling down it; he shouldn't be alive right now. The blood lowers over his eyes and down his cheek.

He leans forward, resting his face in his hands, "I swear, I swear to God, if I could undo this, I would. I promise I would," he begins to sob. It would make more sense if I was hallucinating right now, I think I'm losing too much blood. He shouldn't be walking but I'm more surprised to see him cry. Through his tears he chokes up words, "I know I've done bad things, I know I've done terrible things, but I never meant to hurt anybody."

My anger surfaces helplessly. Suddenly I'm enraged, by body gets a spurt of energy, just enough to raise my shoulder with one hand; not much more. He raises his hands towards me, "Please, just hear me out."

A story went on, rambling my ears off. There's a battle going on while I lie helplessly, listening to the most despicable person possible tell me bedtime stories. Dying doesn't sound too bad right about now.

"The surreals took everything from me, Mason," he said with pain in his eyes. He grabs my leather jacket and pulls me in, "My family. My home. *Everything.*" He lowers his head as well as my body in disdain after a brief pause, "It doesn't make what I did okay, it doesn't justify what I've done." I watch as the wound on his head patches itself up; his skin stitches itself back together and repairs the wound. I can't help but shake my head, this man that I've hated for years, this man that I've frowned upon, cursed, absolutely despised. He's sitting on his knees as I lay on death's doorstep, sobbing his eyes out, spilling his wretched heart all over me.

I don't trust this man at all. He's lying.

"Mr. Parker is a psychopath, Mason," he tells me with broken vocals. His expression sobers, his voice darkens. He points to the bullet wound on his thigh, then the one on his head, "He wants death and he wants power," he coughs up blood on the ground behind him.

My aching chest begins to pulsate, my heart beats harder and harder. Continuing on, he tells me about an evil plot Parker has concocted, a plan to create a new species, "He's going to make an empowered between the ethereal and surreals, one that was more powerful than any other species that has ever faced this Earth," he chokes, "One that he could control." My director's expression is stern but begging, he's asking me for something.

I look behind him in my daze, the giant machines have sustained minimal damage so far but their opponents are worn down. I can feel it deep within myself, Theodore is lying to me. It's too convenient, it can't be this easy. Never would he come to me belly-down and surrender, it's not within him to do so.

"What do you want from me?" I ask him, my voice hoarse and quiet.

His expression grows very serious, very dark, very quickly, "Take my powers from me, Mason. You keep fighting on, Mason, I want you to be the hero here."

I look at him with an amused expression.

"Take my powers from me. Consume my soul, use my powers for yourself. I know what you are, I've known about your powers all along. You'll be healed. Your wounds are superficial, you'll be healed in minutes. You'll be able to fight again, Mason. Take my life, don't you know what I've done to this world, Mason? To you?"

I'm sure I'm falling right into his hands. I'm right where he wants me to be, I have been for a long time, I'm positive.

I can't even comprehend what's going on, I can't even begin to fathom what I'm hearing. I don't know how to respond, I don't know what to do. I've wanted, for so long, nothing more than for this man to be put down, punished for what he did. Now he's asking me to kill him?

My thoughts are flooded, my body is in so much pain I'm going numb. My torso feels like it's going to explode from the pressure building in my chest.

Do it, Mason.

CHAPTER XIX

THE BIGGER THEY ARE, THE HARDER THEY FALL

This man; this fiend to society has killed more people than I'm willing to count and I know for a fact he'd be willing to kill more. I've watched, with my own eyes, Theodore's men kill surreals in cold blood. Maybe this is why I don't trust him, maybe this is why I can't take his pleas seriously. I can't trust any man who doesn't find regret in pulling the trigger.

Killing one of his own.

Do it, Mason!

They're so close together, I can't tell if Anna or Parker is saying it. This ethereal voice has betrayed me so many times, would it be worthy to listen either way?

Rose looks me dead in the eyes before she flies back from the impact of the foot of one of the machines. Logan jumps to her aid but is swatted away, caught by the off-balanced body of his brother. Victoria cries out as one of the monsters pick her up by her ankles. She tries to escape but to no avail.

I can't die here.

I feel my body entombing his mortal existence; worse, I can feel myself healing. I'm slowly killing a man and gaining from his decay. Darkness encases me like a blanket, like a sack over my head, like I can't see. I can hear whispers in my ears.

Part of me wants to let him die. Part of me wants to watch him rot away, watch as he turns into the lifeless corpse he deserves to be. The other part of me is already gone, a small part of me doesn't want to be alive right now. I'm slowly giving my soul back to him, the wasted, decrepit keys that make up my soul; the part of me that's dying.

Normally I feel empowered; like I want to take it all. Not this time. This time I don't want *any* of it, I'd rather have none. Not even the drug of power can persuade me otherwise, I hate this feeling, I hate this guilt, I already regret my actions. My wounds are healing but the pain is just getting worse. I hate this, I hate myself, I hate everything.

I look down at the donor of my sorrow, the one who saved my life after ruining it. I can't tell how I feel when I think this, I don't know how I should, I don't know what it means to me but I know one thing keeps rattling around in my head.

Do it, Mason.

There's no point in fussing, there's no point in wasting anymore time. He's given me something, he's gifted me a curse, a power that I can use to save those I love. I've made a deal with the devil and I'm using my advantages before they destroy me.

I can already tell that he wasn't giving me the full truth. There's more to him than the powers he explained, I'm surging with capability. I have no idea what this man was but he wasn't human.

As I watch his body fall to the ground, I swear I could see him smile.

Battle rages on in front of me, three giant mechanized monsters hit the ground, hit the walls, hit anything they can grasp as lights flare on from the fingertips of young, crippled warriors. Jumping, fighting, flying, everybody is fighting, everybody is at war with each other. Those on the ground are weak, barely holding on to their breaths.

Running at full speed, I give my entire body to my power, one quick leap sends me flying through the air. What's powering me right now; rage? Hatred? Sorrow? I can't tell, my soul is a mess, my emotions are clustered together. There's something coursing through my veins, it's dark and disgusting. I can't tell what's going on. I don't care what's going on.

My shoulder braces itself into a wall of dark glass, cracks form in the blink of an eye. I see Logan's and Jayden's reflection in the shards. The crack I've created reminds me of them; the way they fight together, the brotherhood they hold, the bond they share. The high speeds the fragments fly at remind me of them. They quickly disappear in a cloud of smoke and rubble.

Blood rushes down my skin but in little time I feel relieved, the pain subdues itself before I can even feel it. I climb up before I can fall, shot after shot I strike the machine. Weak points, joints, anything other than flat metal. I give it a hit for every weak spot I find; I see Victoria's reflection in a shiny spot of the tarnished steel. Small, quick strikes where it hurts most, cunning blows. Gut shots and skin pricks, she manipulates the small things that make up a person. It takes courage to use her power the way she does, it takes loss to act out the way she does.

A crack big enough to fit my fist through shows itself; big enough to put both hands in. One finger, two fingers, one hand, eight fingers; I get both hands in facing opposite directions. All my strength, all my mind, all my body; I pull them apart. With everything I have I shear the glass to pieces, revealing the pilot's fleshy body. Behind the mech I see Rose; fear, focus, the most potential I've ever seen. I'm using everything I've got in my artillery. Using brains when they ask for strength, using your wits when there's no muscle left to use.

It shatters. Remnants falls across the field, another pilot is exposed; I fall. Catching myself on his leg, he tries to squirm his way out, kick me off, but to no avail. The robotic arms flail around but nowhere near close enough to make their way to me. It's too late, anyway. With both feet on the steel body, I grip his leg with everything I have and *pull*. Pull his body away from the seat; the buckles snap, the belts rip. The robot stutters to a stop as its controller vacates. Dropping out of the machine, the man flies across the street. We're so high in the air, there's so much shrapnel on the ground. He's not just at the mercy of gravity, he's at the mercy of my strength, the mercy of the power I put into launching him. He's at *my* mercy.

By the time he hits the ground a couple times, another man's blood stains my hands like ink, the most demonic writing I've ever seen. It...

It feels good.

Kicking myself off the machine, I grab a hold of the next target. I can't see its face, I can only see its back. A small slit drives its way down both sides near the arms; damage and corrosion has tilted the corners outwards, created an opening. Using it as my grip, I pry the metal sheet off the back of the mech. A messy tangle of colorful wires show, a jumbled mess of electronics. I don't know what they do, I don't care what they do. I begin tearing and ripping at every last one of them.

What are the others doing? Watching, they're watching me, the monster I'm succumbing to, the demon I've become. Parker is the one doing all the damage, Parker is the one leading the charge. Parker is the one trying to kill all my friends. For the first time, I'm *not* scared. I'm *not* worried. No, I'm angry. Nothing but anger fills my senses, I see, smell, breathe a soothing shade of red.

It's the soul; the soul has done terrible things to me. It's changing me, making me a different person. Somebody I despise, somebody I would never want to be. But the power it's giving me is delicious. I want to *indulge*.

Tearing out wires, I'm destroying whatever I can get my hands on. Looking from side to side I can see thin motors and dangling wires from each arm; I sever all of them. Flailing like crazy, the arms and legs begin to go haywire. They freak out, up and down, side to side, the controller has lost control. Without his consent, the glass casing suddenly starts the process of opening.

134

Stop looking with anger, have a little conscience, think for a second, Mason! Think about what you're doing, who you're hurting. Who you're *killing*.

I'm killing people. I've killed plenty of people. This thought takes hold of me, makes me stop for a brief moment; not for long, though. Only long enough to enjoy my work.

I leap over the glass, into the cockpit of the automation. Sitting in a steel chair lies another pilot, another leader of destruction. I don't have mercy, I don't feel guilt, I feel nothing. I feel an emptiness within myself; I grab him by the collar and rip him from his seat. Another crack of the buckles, another tear of the belts relieves him of his position.

I can feel the machine tilting, it's rocking towards me, it's going to fall. Dropping the man dangling in my hands, I see a look of terror from him. I don't regret anything except not making eye contact with him, I regret missing the look on his face while he falls from my grasps; while he plummets beneath the machine I've destroyed. I'm filling my emptiness with blood.

Jumping away from the wreckage faster than any human could, I left him below the machine as it fell. Too big to show any marks, reveal any blood, give a peek at any splatter marks, the machine did nothing but let us know that the man beneath that giant hunk of steel was to never breathe again.

I pant, I gasp as heavy as my lungs can carry, I stand hunched over my victim. I can't take it, this is destroying me, this is eating me alive. Why don't I care? Why am I like this?

I look forward, the battle has paused, for a brief moment I get a glimpse of everybody staring at me. Parker's mech is stumbling back to regain itself. The smallest moment, the quickest second for everybody to take a quick look at the monster I've become. They're hurt, agonizing, caring about nothing more than staying alive. Nobody cares except Rose.

Rose stands in terror as she watches me, as she listens to my thoughts. Why must she always be peering through me? She doesn't need to see who I am. I'm happy how I am, she'll only ask me to change.

CHAPTER XX

THE COST OF A LIFE

I hate myself. I'm torn and I truly despise myself. I can't decide, I can't end this war I'm having with another half of me. My soul is molded in such an evil, despicable way; a way that I don't want to live with. A way that created the man I've despised my whole life, the type of man who's willing to kill without regrets. I *need* this man now, I need this man I hate, I need a man that I've despised for so long, despised my whole life. This man *is* me, I despise myself. I *hate* myself.

I hate Theodore, I need Theodore Drakone. I hate myself, I need myself.

I don't want to be this sick twisted monster that consumes me, he was lying the whole time, that sick bastard. He knew the whole damn time that I would struggle with this, he knew the whole damn time that what he had was a burden and all he wanted to was to give it to somebody else. I can see why he would want to die, I can see why he wouldn't want to live like this. A terrible life, a terrible look on us all, a terrible perspective to see by.

I feel bad for everybody who has to watch. I'm sorry, Rose, I know you're listening.

The rage, the anger, the torture of being alive entombs the coils that power my legs; with one great leap I make my way to the cockpit of the machine that Mr. Parker is piloting. As soon as our gazes meet we both know where this is going to go. His flailing, his attempts to escape, anything he can do is all pointless. There's no running, there's no mercy to be given.

I wrap my hands around the belt that holds the fiend in front of me strapped into his seat; I don't need to filter any strength into my grip this time. This time, I'm holding on like my life depended on it.

I cock back; I've been here before, memories rush in of moments before, the amount of damage, the amount of destruction I've done with this position. My fist is held back around my ear, blood is dripping down my lips and my fingers, my fist is bloody from the numerous blows it's taken. Pain drowns my emotions, these memories are overwhelming me, internal misery. I feel nothing but hatred, I don't want to be here, I don't want to be in this position. I know they're all watching me, I don't even need to look. I can feel it, they're watching my every movement. This time, I'm in the limelight, I'm the hero and the killer.

The devil wears a suit and tie; he has nice shoes and an icy glare. He offered me a piece of him and I thought I could save everybody with it. Everybody's being saved, aren't they?

Why can't I just enjoy my victory?

I punch Mr. Parker in the jaw. I hear a loud crack as I feel it shatter. Another punch sinks itself into his skin; his ugly, old, wrinkly skin slowly begins to swell and turn brightly colored. Bright purple, dark red, the colors of hatred that will never explain how I feel. Nothing will explain how I feel.

"I hate you," another punch rains down on him. "I hate everything you stand for," another one. "I can't stand you," another.

Punch after punch I can feel the monster inside me getting fed. Every blow I deal to him feeds the hungry monster that will never be satisfied; an everlasting pit of despair inside me. "You're the worst," another punch. "The world is better off without you," again. I can see blood splattered all over his face; it's not even just his own blood.

Feeding it only makes it hungrier; the monster inside me only wants more. A glutton for punishment, a fat monster gorging on pain. I don't want this, I don't need this, this shouldn't be happening; *I don't stop.*

I can see his teeth shattering within his mouth, his nose is growing more and more crooked, his eyes are draining blood. Another punch goes in straight for his nose, "You deserve suffering."

No matter how much I do to him, no matter *what* I do to him, his uncaring expression doesn't change. An expression like that of one who doesn't care, *an icy glare.* He's like the man that plagues my soul, the encryption on the essence of my life that I wish I could get rid of, the curse I want eliminated from my body forever.

"You don't deserve love," another punch reaches his broken nose. "You don't deserve passion," a loud crack reaches my ears as my knuckles make contact with his cheekbone. "You deserve nothing but *agony!*" another punch cripples his face beyond repair.

I don't understand. Nobody understands. I can see myself outside my body, frozen in time; a man with a face beyond repair, broken nose, plump and bright features, eyes and lips and facial features rotated at awkward angles. My leather jacket, my hood, my t-shirt, my pants, all torn and burned and ripped to shreds; every piece of cloth is soaked in blood. Cocked back, my fist is flinging blood as I make desperate eye contact with my target. Around me is destruction, around me is a disgusting trail of violence and misdeeds.

Who am I? What have I become? What has lead me so far astray that I'm willing to take the life of a man, one that I hate or not, a man nonetheless. What has brought me to this point?

This isn't you, Mason.

I know it's not me. I wish I could forget; this isn't me, these aren't my actions, this isn't how I would act. I'm working off the fuel, the emotion, the memories of the most hateful man I've ever met. I hate him, I hate myself.

My conscience floods back. A brief moment of feeling, a brief moment of who I used to be; who I *want* to be. Nothing would feel better right now than being who I was born to be, to live with the soul I was born with. For a brief moment, I can feel it. I can feel myself again.

Mason!

The moment ends. Something's tapping on the walls of my brain, something is tapping on the guarding that makes up my will power. Something's asking... For my consent.

He's taking my soul from me. He's trying to eat away at the wretched soul that comprises my life essence. He's a Striker just like me. Damn it, "*Go ahead and take it!*" I scream as I send out more deadly blows. Somebody will finally relieve me of this bastard's soul but I need to make quick work. He'll start healing faster than I can dish out blows in a second, I need to hit harder, faster, *stronger.*

I know you can do it, Mason. I believe in you!

The voices are jumbled in my head now. I can't tell who's speaking, I don't care who's speaking. Hit him, break his face, destroy him. Annihilate him. This time he's reacting, his expression turned from smug to desperate, he's worried. He's finally scared, he knows he's losing. He's not going to make it at this point. The floodgates of my will are open; wide open. He can have my damned souled, it'll only give me more time to kill him.

Cracking; I hear more and more cracking of bones, it's not just him. My fingers are starting to fracture, the pain is surging through me now. I can feel every bone start brittle up, I focus my energy farther and harder into my fists. All of my energy is getting funneled, what matters right now is the intensity of my hits. More, harder, faster.

Stronger, Mason. Stronger!

He stops. Why did he stop? He has enough space for more soul, how could he quit such an addiction with so much room left? So much power to take. His life is on the edge, his toes are hanging over the end of the cliff. Only one more hit; one more blow would end this whole thing.

He moves his face; slowly he makes his way until he has the one eye that's not swollen shut on me. Brittle cracks hit my ears as he attempts to move his broken bones, healing or not I can feel his pain; he's hurt, he's dying, he's giving up. His last words, the last bit of voice he gets to sputter, "I'm sorry I wasn't there, Mason."

I lower my hand, he's not taking any more soul, he's not thwarting me. His eyes are dull and grey, totally blunt and covered in bruises. Yet, they're so familiar to me, so comforting, "It's my fault you're here." His voice is tattered and horse, he's choking on the words as they come out. "I wish I... Could have..."

He's not healing at all. Before he finishes his last sentence, the life escapes from his eyes.

CHAPTER XXI

MY LAST PAINFUL RESOLVE

Everyone is huddled around, I'm lying on the ground in pain; my body aches, my bones shattered. Everybody has a hint of sadness in their expression but all of them are flooded with relief. It's over, the battle is over. The company has lost its biggest leaders. Who would take rein now? Hopefully somebody with a conscience, hopefully somebody who wants to protect, somebody who truly wants to make the world a better place.

Maybe we can find a home for people like us, maybe we can find a place where we can all be safe. Where those who are different can feel like they're one of many, where we can feel protected. Maybe we can find us all a home.

Jayden and Logan broke from the group to go spend some time healing together; can't blame them, it's been a pretty rough day. They haven't seen each other for half a year and the first reuniting day is near both of their death beds. Some relaxing is totally justified for both of them. Seeing Logan so happy, seeing Jayden so happy, it warms me up a little bit inside.

Apparently the two Flickerers were siblings, twins in fact. The resemblance between them is uncanny. They're really smart; too smart, frankly. Trying to explain their powers to me was a waste of time, I understood little to none of. Looking to my side, Anna was acting like she already knew it all. It didn't make sense, it didn't need to make sense. They decided it would be best if they stayed on the Rogue Street alley, it wouldn't be surprising if more ethereals came like they did, this lust for meeting the others must have been strong within all of us. More will come, we all know it.

Rose, Victoria, and Veronica decided to tour each other around their homes; Veronica comes from a place near here but outside town, walking distance apparently. At the same time, Veronica has never been downtown before a week ago. Together, they decided that it would be nice to show her around for a little bit, get to know the area. Rose always has her phone on her, I trust her enough to keep herself safe enough. Same goes for Victoria and Veronica.

With everyone gone, that left me and Anna walking together around the streets. Something tugged at the back of my head about her but I couldn't put my finger on what it was.

"Do you think there's more than just a voice?" she asked me. I was confused by her question at first. She continues, "Like what if we share a brain, too? What if we share a whole body? It's hard to comprehend what our powers are and what they mean, what we can do beyond reality. It's hard to understand an ethereal power because even though we stand behind it, we see through the lens created by reality; we see through the eyes that a realistic world that's been dropped on us. But what if we don't have to? What if there's a pair of eyes that we all share, what if there's a way that we could all see the same thing *outside* reality?"

As we walk down the street, the sun creates a radiating glimmer off of Anna. After all this time, I still have no idea what her powers are capable of, what exactly they do. She's so mysterious to me. I've seen her in battle, I know she was helping... I guess I just wasn't paying enough attention.

Suddenly, she grabs my hand, squeezing it tightly. Not in a

romantic way but rather with determined eyes. It hurts really bad; my hands are pretty badly injured. At the same time we both yelp, grabbing our hands in pain. Without hesitation, we suddenly make eye contact; she felt what I felt? She's not injured, the hand that's in pain for her wasn't even touched. She's feeling *my* pain, she's feeling what my nerves felt. No, what our hands felt, "See? We do share more."

Talking became normal to us, conversing became easy. It feels like I've known her for so long; perhaps I have. Maybe conversing comes easy to us because we tend to feel the same way. Maybe this brain we share is what makes us so agreeable, so easy to talk to.

Anna knows a lot more than I ever would have expected. In fact, she knew the whole time that she was walking into a trap. She *planned* for it.

Theodore Drakone's reign spans much further than this city; it's more apt to say it covers the globe. His history, his ancestors goes back thousands of years. Her smile is bright and genuine but there's a pain in her eyes, "The pain of knowing," she calls it. It's not the kind of pain you see from a rough childhood, it's the type of pain you feel when putting down a pet. Like she knows that she has to hurt somebody to save somebody.

"You're really important, Mason. I'm not sure if you understand that," she tells me after a long moment of staring at the sunset behind the buildings. "You're very popular in the world of ethereals, you know?"

I'm struck by her words. Popular? "Nobody knows me," I squint at her, "You feeling okay?"

"Not by name," she giggles. "But by power. There's a long line of people like you, Mason. You have a gift. Not a gift like the other ethereals do. Much, much bigger." I tear begins to crawl down her cheek. Her face expresses the moment just before administering a lethal shot to a loved one, "Mason."

I look at her, waiting for her words. She's silent but she's choking something up.

"Mr. Parker..." Anna chokes on her words.

Lightly, I rest my hand on hers, she laces her fingers between mine. It's rather soothing. In fact, it feels really nice. The warmth of her touch makes the wounds feel a little bit better. Her gentle touch makes the pain go away, her eyes makes the hurt disappear. Out of all the things I've seen disappear today, from reality, from one place to the next, from vision, nothing disappeared so smoothly and so swiftly as the stress did when I made eye contact with her. I've seen plenty of really weird things today, but this feeling might just take the cake.

Don't worry about it, we can talk later.

"Do you feel it, too?" she looks at me, she's blushing, now, "The heaviness? The weight on your chest? The pain?"

I can't even respond, I'm absolutely speechless. I look down and around my body. Look at what we've been through, look at what suffering we've gone through to get to this point, look at where we ended up after all. I've been at least three different people today, *literally*. Somehow, I can't help but feel happy that I'm Mason, I can't help but feel ecstatic that I'm with Anna.

I look at her in an attempt to respond but I'm interrupted; something soft, something warm, something pressed up against my lips. Is she kissing me? My mind goes numb, my vision begins to blur a little bit; I close my eyes.

I count the seconds, my breathing feels heavy but I can barely breathe. The feeling is sweet, I smell a light hint of strawberry fighting the odor of gunpowder and smoke. The warm air and cool breeze brushes past me; for once in so long, I'm so happy here.

After what felt like an eternity, her lips detach from mine. I already miss the feeling, I already miss the sensation. Silently, she rests her head on my shoulder. Lightly wrapping my hand in hers, she snuggles up to me. Right now, we're sitting in the exact spot that Robert and I used to sit, the exact same place where I used to see him every day, sitting in a corner between where the wall and the ground meets. It's chilly outside, yet I feel warm.

About an hour of silence we finally decide to get going. She wants to meet the other ethereals, wait to see if more come around. I want to, I want to meet more people like us, more that share the bond we share.

"I'll be right there, I just…" I pause for a second, "This place has a lot of memories for me, I just…" I look around for a brief second, soaking in memories. She nods in agreement She runs off. I feel determination and happiness flood my senses. Am I feeling this from myself or from her? Am I feeling what I'm feeling or what she's feeling?

What we're feeling?

I wish this warmth and the gentle breeze could stay forever. I know it can't, life doesn't work with forevers. Even as an ethereal I know that. Reality has laws, reality lives under strict rules. We're bound to reality, at least for now.

I walk around inspecting the area. I never said it but I'm looking for something specific. Grey Street, the place where Red and I first met, the place where I became the person I am today. The place where I fought, the place where I learned, the place where I experienced life on the streets. This is where all of my happiest moments were; the cycle rages on.

And just as it does, this is the spot where somebody close to me died. Somebody close to my heart.

I turn a corner walking into the alley where I met him. Without warning, I feel a sharp stabbing pain in my stomach. I'm looking over somebody's shoulder. Not just a stabbing pain, not just a cramp, not just an emotional burn; I'm getting stabbed. I can feel a blade, a cold, lifeless blade enter through my midsection, inches from my heart.

It hurts so bad.

I can smell him, I can see his lightly tanned skin and short black hair. I don't understand, everything was going so well, everything was about to end perfectly, everything was going to be the way I wanted it to be. I was going to be happy. Happy with the *family* I made.

I hear a whisper in my ear, a cold voice with a slightly Spanish accent, "Doesn't feel good, does it? Now two people will know what it feels like; the hatred. The burning hunger for more, the lust for blood. The endless amount of days that I hate myself, the lust for blood." He begins to turn the blade a bit, the sting intensifies, "If I could change, I would, Mason."

His voice hurts more than the blade; I can feel the blood rushing down my skin. I can feel myself dying, why is he still alive? I killed him, didn't I? I thought I would have rid him of his life. I thought I killed four people today.

"You only killed three, Mason," he begins to twist the knife even further. The pain leaves me speechless, fear, agony, torture; it's all too familiar. "You killed a manager of the Vancouver District," he jerks the knife up. I can feel the warmth from my blood spilling, "The VP of the company," another great jerk painfully eats away my flesh, "and you killed your father."

Mr. Parker?

What have I done? As blood drains from my lips I grimace. I knew he was lying to me. I knew he was lying the whole time.

I knew he was lying.

EPILOGUE

ANASTASIA

I can feel it, I feel it in my heart, in my mind; I feel it throughout my whole body. As of minutes ago, 12 ethereals walked the Earth. At the beginning of the day, it was 14. Gavin's death reaped us of one, the death of Mr. Parker, father of Mason Parker, reaped us a second. Why is it fading, what's going on? Is somebody in trouble?

Mason, what's going on?

I can't feel a reply, I can't feel anything. Instead, I feel my life draining from me; it feels like there's blood dripping down my chest but my shirt has no stains; my chest is sealed. Slowly, with agony in my heart, I can feel as one more ethereal is relieved from existence.

I may be standing the farthest back, and nobody may agree with me, but I know I'm crying the hardest. Maybe not on the outside, but on the inside.

Two weeks ago today, exactly 14 days, Mason was killed.

Eight people surround the coffin, his name carved into the laminated redwood surface. Slowly, the casket is lowered into a deep hole in the ground with a small blue rose, its light petals the color of the sky. Everybody is somber, the mood dark and depressed. Everybody is sad, huge tears crawwl down Jayden's cheeks, Victoria is trying confidently to fight her screaming emotions but it's obvious how devastated she is. Rose is bawling her eyes out, sadness overwhelms her, she can't even control herself.

They don't even know the half of it. Mason wasn't just a mentor to the kids or some shoulder for the crying. He was the most powerful out of all of us. We can't end this without him.

He was murdered in cold blood by Theodore Drakone. He's just like me, burdened with knowledge and a lineage, a powerful opinion, to defend.

Drakone has a special power that no other empowered has; a talent called domination. A mental bond is created between him and another, he can not only steal power but control others with this bond. Normally, this is only limited to another single mortal but technology has made his ability much more advanced. Using the broad networking Dragon Technology uses for their cellular devices, he's able to keep chambers full of surreals waiting for his beckoning call.

Mason's death could mean the end of humans.

Three more ethereals have shown up since our call, we've sent out more and more messages in an attempt to try to get as many as possible. There are six ethereals in our party now, only five left around the world. I can feel them tugging at me, begging me to get closer. Half-ethereals or not, they're there. They're searching.

There's a larger being here, some huge body that all ethereals share in common. I think there's even more to it, I think there's a million things yet to be discovered. I want to learn but our chances dropped when Mason died. Dragon Technology Incorporated has allowed the public some insight on who we are but not enough to get themselves burned.

Tears well up in my eyes when I think about the way Mason pulled me closer; the warmth of his body and the connection we share turning us into the strongest magnets in the world. All we could do is get closer, all we could do is stay together forever. The ethereal connection is stronger than in bond, we can get closer to each other than any mortal can.

All of us together, hand and hand, we vow to make sure that nobody else gets hurt, we vow that this reign of terror comes to an end. We swear that we will avenge those we've lost and make amends for what has happened to this world, we will make the world a better place for every species that steps foot on it.

Nobody knows that I'm lying; nobody but Rose.

"For Mason," I say; our hands are joined, I can feel the connection we share. It's tarnished, hurt by the past.

I hear a chorus of voices, the cries of my new brothers and sisters, *"For Mason!"*

Printed in the United States
By Bookmasters